ELIZA WHEATON
BOOK ENDOWMENT FUND

Eliza Frances Wheaton Strong   Eliza Baylies Chapin Wheaton

Made possible by generous gifts to the

WHEATON COLLEGE LIBRARY

Norton, Massachusetts

"as the sun sets Mosco announces his promesa to give up drinking (perhaps, he tells himself, he has been responsible for other milagros throughout San Miguel. Earlier that day he had heaved a brick through the front window of La Golondrina and an empty bottle into the windshield of a classic Thunderbird down at Madman Martínez's Car Lot), inspiring him not only to make a pilgrimage across the wide llano, but to make it on his knees."

—from "La Promesa"

Welcome to the *other* San Miguel, a fictional town in New Mexico. It's the sort of town that has survived a burning rosary, the face of Jesus appearing on a wall, a sixteen-foot rattler, Mosco Zamora's repeated promises to stop drinking ("No drinking. Absolutamente"), a new doctor who brings a woman back from the dead, a tow-truck driver who wins the demolition derby every Saturday night, María Martínez's WORLD-FAMOUS macaroons, the worst roads in the state, and the fractured dreams of a boy who was sent to Vietnam.

This collection of short stories by Leroy V.

La Promesa
and Other Stories

CHICANA & CHICANO VISIONS OF THE AMÉRICAS

La Promesa

AND

Other Stories

Leroy V. Quintana

UNIVERSITY OF OKLAHOMA PRESS · NORMAN

ALSO BY LEROY V. QUINTANA

Hijo del Pueblo: New Mexico Poems (Las Cruces, 1976)

Sangre (Las Cruces, 1981)

Interrogations (Tucson, 1990)

The History of Home (Tempe, 1993)

(ed., with Virgil Suarez and Victor Hernández Cruz)
Paper Dance: 55 Latino Poets (New York, 1995)

My Hair Turning Gray among Strangers (Tempe, 1996)

The Great Whirl of Exile (Willimantic, Conn., 1999)

Library of Congress Cataloging-in-Publication Data

Quintana, Leroy.
    La promesa and other stories / Leroy V. Quintana
        p.   cm. — (Chicana & Chicano visions of the Américas ; v. 1)
    ISBN 0–8061–3449–6 (hardcover : alk. paper)
    1. New Mexico—Social life and customs—Fiction.   2. Vietnamese Conflict, 1961–1975—New Mexico—Fiction.   3. World War, 1939–1945—New Mexico—Fiction.   4. Hispanic Americans—Fiction.   I. Title.   II. Series.

PS3567.U365 P76 2002
813'.54—dc21

                                                                                            2002017307

La Promesa and Other Stories is Volume 1 in
the Chicana & Chicano Visions of the Américas series.

The paper in this book meets the guidelines for permanence and durability of the Committee on Production Guidelines for Book Longevity of the Council on Library Resources. ∞

1   2   3   4   5   6   7   8   9   10

*Para Sra. y Sr. Nina y Guillermo Holguin, who told me some
of these stories, which inspired me to write
when I was young and to search for my roots and myself.*

Y para Yolanda, Sandra, Elisa, y José

Contents

Acknowledgments

"And on All Your Children"
was published in *Currents from the Dancing River:*
Contemporary Latino Fiction, Nonfiction, and Poetry,
edited by Ray González. New York: Harcourt Brace, 1994.

"The Best Bourbon"
was published in *My Hair Turning Gray among Strangers,*
Leroy V. Quintana. Tempe: Bilingual Press, 1996.

"La Promesa"
was published in *Pleiades,* Vol. 15, Number 1, Fall 1994,
Department of English and Philosophy,
Central Missouri State University, Warrensburg.

"The Rosary"
was published in *Mirrors beneath the Earth:*
Short Fiction by Chicano Writers, edited by Ray González.
Willimantic, Conn.: Curbstone Press, 1992.

Mosco

The Rosary

It was on the last evening of Doña Matilda's novena to St. Jude, the patron saint of the impossible, that Mosco saw the burning rosary on the wall and ran out of the house, stark raving naked, all the way across San Miguel, and burst into church shouting "¡Milagro! ¡Milagro! ¡Milagro!" claiming he would never again taste another drop of wine as several women fainted in the middle of a "Padre Nuestro" and Father Schmidt, who had survived such milagros as the face of Jesus on a tortilla and on the wall of the iglesia, began running alongside Mosco, trying desperately to cover his front, his back, his front with the small prayerbook, screaming "¡Ave María Purísima! ¡Ave María Purísima! ¡Ave María Purísima!" dismissing the faithful with a haphazard sign of the cross as he shoved Mosco into the confessional, and Mosco, not wanting to be disrespectful, immediately made the sign of the cross and began: "Bless me, Father. I had just undressed. I've been meaning to fix that switch. I was going to take a bath. A terrible day, absolutely. You have to turn the light OFF to turn it ON, so I flipped the switch to OFF and all I see is chispas flying everywhere, so I flipped it ON to turn it OFF, and when I flipped it OFF again the lights wouldn't come on, and that's when I saw it, a rosary burning on the wall. ¡Milagro! ¡Milagro!" And when Father Schmidt inquired, "Have you been drinking, my son?" Mosco admitted sheepishly, "Well, yes, Father. One little tragito. Only one. Absolutely. You see, I made a promesa, absolutely."

But I should begin at the beginning, that morning when Mosco realized he had put off getting his driver's license renewed as he'd put off the lawn, the fence, the faucets, the blinkers, the roof. "Una desgracia," Matilda said every morning, and she was right; she was absolutely right. The sockets in the bathroom. And now he had to take the driving test, and that meant taking a little time off from work and putting up with Sapo Sánchez's lecture on driving for the greater part of an hour.

After calling and informing Chango Vásquez, the foreman at the mine, that he would not be in (agreeing that he had been taking too much time off lately, absolutely, and reassuring Chango that this was not going to happen again, and after agreeing with Matilda that he had—she was right, absolutamente—been taking too much time off lately and reassuring her that it was not going to happen again, and after promising, "None, no. No drinking. Absolutamente."), Mosco drove downtown, all the way absolutely convinced that the absolutely perfect way to begin a day that was going to begin with Sheriff Sapo Sánchez was with a chilled swallow, just a little tragito of Wild Irish Rose or Mogen David down at La Golondrina with Botas Meadas and Dupo. But a promesa was a promesa, absolutely. ▪

"Your blinkers," Sapo said immediately, indicating there was no need to proceed any further than the first item on his safety checklist. "Two Sixty-Five Point One of the State Code. No driver's examination to be conducted until vehicle has passed all safety checks. Period." What the town of San Miguel did not need was another Caruso Zamora. ▪

All the way to Caruso's Garage, Mosco was more than absolutely convinced that the perfect way to begin a day that began with Caruso would be to stop off at La Golondrina. . . . Pero, no. No. Absolutely no drinking. A promesa was a promesa was a promesa. Absolutely. ▪

Caruso, the undisputed champion of the demolition derby Saturday night after Saturday night, was under a Jeep accompanying himself with a large ballpeen hammer. "Bésame, bésame muchooooo." No, he couldn't get to the blinkers right now. "Fifteen minutes," he said as he jumped into the tow truck and sped off for parts. "Your cheatin' heeaaaart . . ." ▪

"Your brights," snapped Sapo immediately. No use proceeding beyond the second item. "Two Sixty-Five Point One." ▪

The best way, absolutely, to begin to save a morning that led from Sapo to Caruso, back to Sapo, and then back to Caruso was to stop at La Golondrina, just one chilled tragito of Wild Irish Rose or Mogen David. But just one. After all, a promesa . . ." ▪

"Acuérdate de Acapulco . . ." Caruso was bent over the heart of a Coupe de Ville, pounding a large screwdriver into the defenseless carburetor. "Not now . . . fifteen minutes. María Bonita, María del almaaaa . . ." ▪

"Back in fifteen. My rooose, my rooose of San Antoooooneo . . ." Fifteen turned into twenty. Caruso rocketed back into his parking space, the tow truck lurching to a stop as he jumped from his seat. "All the waaay. She sent it to her lover who was airborne all the way!" He was sorry for the delay. El Cabrón del Sapo and his espeeding tickets; the same boring lecture over and over. "Yeah, I know which law I'm breaking. Three Seventy-One Point Three. Espeeding. ¿Y qué? Now bluuue ain't the word for the waaay that I feeeel." ▪

"Los wipers," snorted Sapo, removing his drill-sergeant hat to wipe his fat brow with his cuff. All this work was making him hungry, mighty hungry. He flipped his dark sunglasses to check his wristwatch. Coffee break in thirty minutes. Hungry. Mighty hungry. ▪

The best way, absolutely, was to stop off . . . a tragito, one, a promesa was absolutely. ▪

"Mis wipers," Mosco intoned.

Caruso put down the crescent wrench he had been hammering with. "From a jack to a queen! Not now . . . fifteen minutes. From loooneliness to a wedding riiiing." ▪

"Coffee break," barked Sapo. "Come back in fifteen minutes. State regulations say an employee is entitled to one fifteen-minute break in the A.M. and one in the P.M. Period." ▪

How could two bowls of menudo, a half-dozen tortillas, two tamales, a slice of apple pie (à la mode), and two cups of coffee . . . a coffee break? Absolutamente, a promesa was a promesa, and stop off at La Golondrina . . . ▪

"Okay," snapped Sapo, "let's roll." Chins trembling, fresh grease stains down his shirt and official black tie. ▪

Now, first was second and . . . no, no. Second was first and third was second, reverse was third. Absolutely. Or was it first was reverse? Second was first, third was second, reverse third . . . no, no. A third tragito had been absolutely out of the question, absolutely. Good thing, otherwise . . . "I'm citing you for a Two Eighty-Nine Point Three, Mosco. Operating an unsafe vehicle." ▪

"My transmission, Caruso."
"Hoy, no," replied Caruso, the sledge hammer high over his head. He burst into song on the downswing: "¡Aaayyy que laureles tan verdeeees! Si pienas abandonarme, mejor quitar me la vidaaaa . . ." ▪

What was absolutely necessary, absolutely, was a new car—or better yet, the image of owning a new car. A quick stop at La Golondrina before driving down to Madman Martínez's Car Lot. A quick tragito or two, chilled. ▪

Why buy a car when, after wrestling with figures with Maxie Baca (the mayor's greedy brother-in-law) for an hour and a half, you could take it out for a test (!) drive, say you're thinking of buying on the deferred payment plan—a good deal, absolutely . . . ▪

"Lunchtime!" bellowed Sapo. Hungry. Mighty hungry. "State regulations . . ." ▪

Lunch? An enchilada special—extra sour cream and avocado, a side order of menudo, a tamale. Time enough to return the car, haggle with Maxie over the price, get another to test drive, stop off behind La Golondrina for a tragito, just one, by the time Sapo slurped up the last of his apple pie (à la mode) and his fourth cup of coffee. ▪

"Weren't you operating a green car a while ago, Mosco?"
"Traded it in."
"Get a good deal?"
"Damn good deal."
"Let's roll." Chins trembling, fresh grease stains. ▪

"I will be asking you to execute various maneuvers such as parking, backing up, proper signaling, proper lane changes . . ."
"¿Qué?"
"I said I will be asking you. . . . Ummhhh, let's begin by backing out. Place your left hand at twelve o'clock and your right arm over the seat, checking continuously for approaching vehicles, checking . . ."
"¿Qué?"
"Accelerating slowly, SLOWLY!" ▪

"Proceed in an easterly direction for two blocks, then execute a right after coming to a proper stop. No honking to greet other motorists. Keep both hands on the wheel at all times, constantly scanning. No smoking during testing. All mirrors should be adjusted prior to testing. No loud music that might prevent you from hearing oncoming or passing motorists. ▪

"Pay no attention to motorists who blow their horn. As long as you are observing the speed limit . . ."

"It's Caruso. He's trying to pass."

"I'm gonna throw the book at that son of a bitch. That's a Two Seventy-One Point Nine, following too close. Stop this car." ■

"Follow that truck, Mosco! I'm throwing the book at that son of a bitch. Crossing the yellow line, a Two Thirty-Four Point Seven; especeding. That's a . . . FOLLOW THAT TRUCK, MOSCO!"

"¿Qué?" ■

". . . that's a Three Seventy-One Point. . . . GO! ¡Accelerate, hombre, accelerate!"

"¿Qué?"

"Step on it, pendejo! Oh, I'm throwing the book . . ." ■

"Turn, Mosco! Turn!"

"But it's against the law."

"Make a U-turn, goddammit. I'm nailing him for a Two Twenty-Two Point Two!" ■

"But it's a one way, Sapo!"

"I don't give a shit! Follow that son of a bitch. That's a Two Nineteen Point Three!" ■

"He's coming back this way!"

"Turn, pendejo, turn!" ■

"Chinga'o, it happened so fast. First the mailbox and then the picket fence and Sapo yelling 'Stop! Stop!' and then slamming on the brakes, sideswiping the giant cottonwood and skidding—in slow motion it seemed at the time—toward the swimming pool, but actually going pretty goddamned fast, como los kamikazes, or like one of those jets when it misses the aircraft carrier, and then coming to a stop, half the car over the water, the back half on dry land, sweet dry land, and then Sapo opening the door, thinking he could inch his way out I guess, and the car dipping, beginning to plunge como un submarine, o como El Titanic, and Sapo hollering that he didn't know how to swim. 'Help! Help!' As if I could help him—hell, I don't know how either—and then María Martínez, Mrs. Mayor, comes out shrieking because we've splashed water all over the papers on the table where the mayor was working, 'The budget! The audit!' All the figures he had been up all night manip-ulating smeared all to hell, and now they didn't know how they were going to bullshit their way past the government auditor, and 'My begonias! My greenhouse!' ¡Chinga'o! I hadn't realized we had plowed right through it, and then she's screaming for the mayor to call the sheriff, but Sapo is clinging to the mayor, trying to tell her that the sheriff has already arrived, and I'm clinging to Sapo until finally María Martínez flips us the lifesaver and the mayor manages to cling on to it while María Martínez fishes Sapo and me out by hooking that long aluminum pole under his gun-belt and tugging like a harpooner, then giving Sapo mouth-to-mouth, me and the mayor are barely walking the road of the liv-ing, and suddenly she's throwing up because Sapo has coughed up the enchilada special with extra sour cream and avocado, the menudo, the tamale, and the apple pie (à la mode), and half an hour or so later Caruso is pulling the car out of the pool and Sapo is explaining to the mayor why he was going the wrong way on a one-way street and the mayor is shouting right in his face, 'You don't break the law to enforce the law, pendejo. I'm taking all this out of your budget,' and all Sapo can say is, 'Yes, sir! Yes, sir! Yes, sir!' and when the mayor is through with him he squeezes in behind the wheel of his official car that his puto of a brother-in-law and faithful deputy Ratón Montoya came driving up in, siren wailing, lights flashing like down at Madman Martínez's Car Lot, and he yells at me to get in, asks me where I need to go and I tell him to see Maxie Baca down at Madman Martínez's Car Lot, where I explain the whole thing to Maxie and he begins punching figures on his adding machine, double checks them, and then hands me the contract and I sign on the dotted line, deferred payment plan—absolutely the worst day, worse than yesterday with the tax auditor, and to top it all off, if this ain't the shits, I flunked the driving exam.

"Te digo, I would've been better off showing up for work. I should've stopped off here first thing this morning for one, just one chilled tragito of Wild Irish Rose, just one stop at La Golondrina, start and end right there because a promesa is a promesa—right, Botas Meadas?—absolutely. You've made a promesa or two in your lifetime, tú sabes, you know what I'm talking about. A promesa, absolutamente, simón, sí, absolutamente one more tragito, but only one—la del estribo—for the road, but just a little one, a promesa is a promesa you know, absolutely." ▪

Except for Matilda and her family, the entire town gathered around Mosco's house within half an hour. The faithful (including the women who had fainted in church) knelt, holding candles, praying rosary after rosary. The skeptics, of course, congregated in the rear, argued, placed bets.

At two A.M. Father Schmidt arrived (finally), with Monsignor Chávez, who had driven the sixty miles from Albuquerque in a time that made even Caruso shudder with envy only to see the newest miracle of modern science: a luminous rosary Matilda had purchased earlier that day and hung on the wall that evening before walking to church to pray to St. Jude, who, perhaps on this, the last evening of her novena . . .

¿Cuáles Burros?

¡Chinga'o! Just because the tejanos were buying up every square inch of San Miguel, legally and especially illegally, didn't mean he was going to stand by and watch them steal his, beginning with the strip of land his family had allowed everybody to use as a road ever since anybody could remember. It was a valuable piece of land because it was the only way in and out of the Cañón de San Miguel. If it fell into Billy Joe's hands . . .

But if Clemente Sosa was going to lose his land, then he was going to lose it his way—¡a chingasos, chinga'o! ▪

The tejano, a fellow who called himself Billy Joe Crawford, had purchased, legally and illegally, the acreage adjacent to the north side of the road and was now claiming the road as his property. He had hired Raymundo Martínez, Esq., to represent him, and it looked like he had enough money to keep Raymundo busy on this case alone for years, appeal after appeal.

And Clemente—what choice did he have but old Pete O'Brien García, who had been a tail gunner in World War II and drank a lot of rye whiskey but nevertheless knew some law and, more importantly, knew not only how to keep crafty lawyers as well as opposing judges off balance.

Clemente knew any kind of legal counsel didn't come cheaply, so he arranged to pay O'Brien García off with parcels of land. ▪

O'Brien García's first move was quite simple, but it was a piece of genius. The court ruled that because Clemente's strip of land had always been used as a road, it had to remain a road—even though it still belonged to Clemente. Clearly, Raymundo had a lot of political clout.

O'Brien García said, "Hell—if it's your road, set up a gate at the entrance and lock it. Use as many chains and locks as you like. Give keys to whomever you like. Then we'll go back to court and see what happens."

The court ruled against Clemente. So then O'Brien García said, "If it's still your road, then put a gate at the other end so Billy Bob can't get in or out of his property. Give keys to whomever you like." He handed Clemente a paper claiming another half acre and emptied a shot of cheap rye. "Lawyers. Chinga'o," Clemente said, signed it, and downed his shot. "Hell, screw Billy Joe and the horse he rode in on. I'm a landowner, too," O'Brien García said. ▪

The court ruled Clemente couldn't put a locked gate at the opposite end of the road, where it dropped down into the cañón. Billy Joe (as well as any other landowner) was entitled to enter and leave his property at any time, unimpeded. Furthermore, Billy Joe's (as well as any other landowner's) life might be placed in danger. "What if," Judge Henry W. Longfellow asked, "an emergency— say, a fire—occurred, and let's say it occurred late at night. Mr. Martínez's client would be denied the services of the fire department. Incidentally, let the court make it quite clear that no such type fire shall or will occur. Case is dismissed." ▪

"If it's your road," O'Brien García said, "and you can't put gates at either end of the road, and nobody said a goddamned thing about putting them anywhere in between, hell—put up all the gates you want, as many as you can afford. Borrow them if you have to. Every hundred feet. Every fifty feet. Or so."

"Every hundred yards. Or so," Clemente said as he signed away another half acre. O'Brien García poured himself another shot from the decanter, and one for Clemente. It went down quite smoothly. A better brand than the fucking lawyer usually offered, Clemente thought. ¡Chinga'o! ▪

Surprisingly, the court ruled the gates could stay. All twenty-five of them. Raymundo filed an appeal.

"If you want the gates to stay," O'Brien García said, "you need to create a situation that'll make them forget about the gates. Hell, make them even appreciate them. Dig some trenches, two or three between each gate. Deep enough so that Billy Joe can't plow his big Cadillac through." He poured a shot of rye for himself and then one for Clemente.

Smooth! An even better brand of rye than the last.

"Of course," he continued, "I won't be able to drive my new Cadillac through either, but hell . . ."

A Cadillac! ¡Chinga'o! ■

"Erosion control, Your Honor," O'Brien García stated. "These trenches allow for controlled runoff during the summer rains. In addition these trenches will provide adequate shelter for much of the animal life of San Miguel County."

Billy Joe was furious. He was through with these bush-league shenanigans! Raymundo appeared nervous. He was about to be demoted. O'Brien García, on the other hand, was looking prosperous. A new suit, new briefcase.

Clemente appeared nervous. ¡Chinga'o! At this rate he'd be out of land soon. Judge Henry W. Longfellow did not allow the trenches. Case dismissed. ■

"Now pay attention, Clemente. Whenever I or Raymundo or the judge or the new hired gun, Jim Bob Harris—hell if I care if he *was* starting halfback for SMU—ask you anything—anything, all you say is, '¿Cuáles burros?' Got it?"

"¿Cuáles burros?"

"Exactly." ■

Raymundo Martínez: "Are you aware, Mr. Sosa, that you have repeatedly placed my client's life in danger?"

Clemente Sosa: "¿Cuáles burros?"

Raymundo Martínez: "Are you aware, Mr. Sosa, that you are being a hostile witness?"

Clemente Sosa: "¿Cuáles burros?"

Raymundo Martínez: "For the last time, Mr. Sosa, do you deny that you deliberately and maliciously placed my client's life in danger? I have made you aware of the penalty for perjury, so please answer truthfully."

Clemente Sosa: "¿Cuáles burros?" ■

Judge Henry W. Longfellow: "Mr. Sosa, are we to believe that you are standing behind the Fifth Amendment?"

Clemente Sosa: "¿Cuáles burros? Your Honor?"

Judge Henry W. Longfellow: "Mr. Sosa, are you then implying that you are entering a plea of insanity?"

Clemente Sosa: "¿Cuáles burros? Your Honor?" ■

Jim Bob Harris wisely chose not to ask any questions. He would settle this issue in a gentlemanly manner. Out of court. ■

"Well, now that Billy Joe and I are vecinos," O'Brien García said, "I suppose I should invite him and his barristers for an old-fashioned barbecue and some conversation—see if we can put an end to this issue in a gentlemanly manner."

"Nobody wants this to end more than I do," Clemente said. He wasn't losing the war, but he wasn't winning it either. Chinga'o. And now O'Brien García was drinking imported rye. ■

Clemente drove to The Emporium and purchased two reels of fishing line. Then he stopped by Mosco Zamora's place and looked at a couple of old bus seats Mosco had rescued from El Dompe Viejo. He made sure the springs were well worn and then paid Mosco. Then he drove to Albuquerque, where he purchased a pickup load of baskets. Then he stopped at every toy store in town.

Maybe he was going to lose most or all of his land, but he sure was going to put one hell of a scare into Billy Joe, along with Raymundo Martínez and Jim Bob Harris, attorneys-at-law. ■

Two days later, at about six in the evening, Billy Joe and his lawyers walked up to Clemente's house. O'Brien García was tending the beef and pouring the imported rye. The talk was gentlemanly. Passing comments on the weather, the rising cost of raising cattle, the rocketing prices of real estate.

Clemente made sure there was plenty of beef, beans, corn on the cob, and potato salad stacked on every plate. And plenty more piled high on top of the kitchen table. No glass was permitted to remain empty.

Then talk, more detailed now, of the rising cost of raising cattle, the current real-estate market. If anything, prices were going to escalate before they went down, so a person would be wise to hold out. On the other hand, the time to sell was now; who knew how things would be in three months, six, a year?

Then Billy Joe began talking about what price he would be willing to pay. He was looking for some property he could develop. Heck, he didn't want no legal quarrels. He was lookin' to be a good neighbor. Heck, he'd have Jim Bob and Raymundo draw up some papers right here and now if it would put an end to any feudin'.

Clemente said "¿cuáles burros?" and when the laughter died down he agreed that when real estate was ridiculously high, friendship went out the window. What was important was for vecinos to get along. Why go on bickering? All they were doing was making lawyers rich. Sure, why not have Jim Bob and Raymundo draw up some papers and settle any bad business.

Jim Bob rifled through some papers in his briefcase, penciled in some figures, and handed them over to Billy Joe. Billy Joe leafed through them, licking his finger to turn them over, nodded his approval, and affixed his signature. He handed them over to O'Brien García, who read them and handed them to Clemente. Clemente read the document slowly, grunting his approval at the end of each paragraph, and, just like Billy Joe, wet the tip of his finger to turn each page.

It looked like he was just about ready to sign when he yelled, "What the hell is this? Just what kind of mierda is this? I'm not gonna sign this!" He balled the papers up, grabbed the shotgun from under the sink, tossed the papers into the air, and—along with blowing them to bits—blasted a hole in the ceiling.

"Now," he said, "what I did to those papers I'm going to do to whoever wrote them and/or signed them if the parties of the first party aren't off the aforementioned property in thirty seconds."

Clemente inserted two new shells into the chambers and flicked the shotgun closed and fired a volley as Raymundo, Billy Joe, and Jim Bob ducked out the front door. Clemente reloaded. Billy Joe and his lawyers were heading towards the road—just as Clemente had planned. Clemente fired again. "¡Ladrones!" he yelled. ▪

Every time Billy Joe or one of his lawyers tripped a fish line, a box would spring six feet or so into the air and a flock of snakes, real ones with buzzing rattlers and rubber ones (in the approaching darkness it was difficult to tell which was which) would rain down on them.

Raymundo was going over the gates quickly and steadily. Billy Joe was right behind him, snakes raining heavily on both of them. And Jim Bob was blazing through O'Brien García's property, sidestepping, skipping, hopping, hurdling, and long-stepping over snakes as if he were heading for the goal line to clinch the win in the last seconds of the darndest Cotton Bowl ever.

And if that wasn't enough to keep them unnerved, well, you can imagine how they sprang out of their chairs and over their desks the following morning when they opened their briefcases that O'Brien García had delivered on behalf of his client, the defendant, thereafter known as "¿Cuáles Burros?"

Mosco Zamora and the
Sixteen-Foot Rattler

Everybody was certain it was La Wedding Bells, who was either next in line or else was in the other confessional, ear pressed to window, who first heard Mosco explain everything—from the time he first saw the rattler to his vacation in Paris—to Father Schmidt. It's quite possible that Sheriff Sapo Sánchez was sitting in the pew right in front of the confessional. Now I would tend to believe Mosco before I took to heart anything that La Wedding Bells or Sheriff Sapo Sánchez said, but that certainly doesn't mean that any, or all I am about to tell you, is the truth. Keep in mind that Mosco was the first to see El Hombre sin Cabeza, the Headless Man, who would one day walk out of the darkness into the head-lights of his son's rebuilt, customized, cherry-red Thunderbird, leaving the son in tears for days and days. It's certain that a few details, facts, or confabulations were added here and there to all three accounts. You know how life in these small towns is. All I can say is that by the time I heard the story it went something like this:

Mosco Zamora yanked off the extra-strength reading glasses he had purchased at The Emporium during María Martínez's (wife of the Honorable Raymundo Martínez, mayor of San Miguel) annual GOING OUT OF BUSINESS SALE, wiped them quickly on the lapel of his suit jacket (this was Sunday, and he was walking home from Mass), guided them up, down, up, down his somewhat long, sharp nose to find the strongest focus possible in order to con-firm what he thought he had seen or imagined (these days the bottles of Wild Irish Rose seemed to empty themselves more and more easily) winding its way down the bottom of the Farnsworth

Arroyo. He could already see the inch-and-a-half banner in María Martínez's *San Miguel Tribune,* followed quickly that same afternoon by the tall, bold headlines in *The Albuquerque Tribune:* "Sixteen-Foot Rattler Found!"

And just below each headline, in print he didn't have to squint to read: "Rattles as Big as Baseballs," along with his picture taking up more of the front page than el pendejo del Ike that los Americanos pendejos had elected as their president, playing golf as usual while the poor worked like burros to put frijoles and tortillas on the table.

Once *The Albuquerque Tribune* printed the story, no telling how much he could (and would) charge María Martínez for the hide and rattles. He was tired of being poor. His monthly government check could be stretched only so far, and all he wanted out of life now was to take a trip to Paris. Nothing fancy, but certainly not on an overcrowded troop train like the first time he had visited there. He wanted to see it one last time. He had longed to see it for so many years—painful years made even more painful by the thought that he would never see it again. It had been impossible with the stingy chickenshit check the government sent him every month as a reward for nearly getting his head cut off by an alemán who had sharpened his bayonet to the deadliest edge possible.

He had seen the bayonet slicing away at his throat every single night since that time the Germans had crawled up the mountain, slowly, slowly, long after each side had run out of ammunition and hurled their last grenades at one another. At about three in the morning, the darkest part of the night, the hand-to-hand fighting began, bayonet against bayonet, clawed hand against clawed hand, reaching for a throat—in order to stay alive, stay alive one more minute until, finally, it would be over, another chapter in the book of hell completed—clawing a pair of eyes out of their sockets, tearing off an ear or two or else snapping a neck, swinging an entrenching tool against clubs fashioned from the remains of trees destroyed by the never-ending, relentless shrill whistle of artillery that had reduced the mountain to three city blocks of hell—a hell so dangerous and haunted the devil himself could not have lived through it. ■

Every night he was awakened by the raging face of the German he had stabbed in the eye with his bayonet before ramming it into his heart with little effect, forcing him to take the young soldier's entrenching tool from him and swing wildly, desperately. When daylight finally arrived and the sergeant lifted the body from Mosco's chest, Mosco, who had come too close to having his head sliced neatly from his body, realized he had killed a handsome young boy of eighteen. It had been hard to tell his age because his face was completely covered with mud. The rain had fallen ceaselessly that entire haunted night, and the entire world was buried in four feet of mud. Ambulances were stuck in mud that in some places seemed ready to swallow them. It had taken three days to get the wounded off the hill.

After getting up and downing a pint of Wild Irish Rose, Mosco would be able to sleep for what seemed a minute, a short minute, until the eyes, the bulging eyes, unmoving and accusing, the eyes that belonged to the head he had chopped off with the entrenching tool, wound their way into his dreams until he awoke. And then not even the three pints he had bought to drown or soothe or perhaps end his suffering would allow him sleep or peace.

The young soldier had on him a picture of what must have been his wife, an orchid blooming in the voracious, blood-sucking mud. One of the men on burial detail had walked over to Mosco and slid it into Mosco's shirt pocket. He had protected it the rest of his time in Europe, and when he finally got home he had wrapped it in a special towel, along with his medals and discharge papers, and placed it underneath his shirts in the bottom drawer of his ancient, pockmarked bureau. Somehow he had made the horror seem meaningful, though he knew he would never ask for nor be given any explanation for one or all of the lives he or anybody else had taken.

If only there had been a way to ask her for forgiveness. Countless times he had taken her picture with him to Mass, next to his heart, and had prayed silently for her, hoping she was alive and well, perhaps enjoying her grandchildren. She was sure to be uttering a prayer throughout the day, doomed to wonder the rest of her days about the fate of the man she loved, the man she had sent off to war aboard a train jammed full of soldiers with a foreboding kiss and bitter tears. ▪

Mosco's unit had trudged on from Paris to the west, where the fighting had grown more and more fierce, where the casualties on both sides were outrageously high. He had spent six months in Paris in a basement of a former shoe store that had been converted into a hospital and then was loaded on a ship bound for home. He had launched into one ocean of tokay after another the minute he was able to slip out of the hospital and pound the streets of New York, utterly lost, in search of one more bottle, a minute's peaceful sleep. He was finally sent home, and since then not a day had gone by that he had not emptied enough cheap tokay to poison himself. And now he was beginning to realize his memory was getting harder to chase down. He was plagued with confusion. He was getting stopped by Sheriff Sapo Sánchez more and more for driving on the wrong side of the road (twice), failure to stop at a stop sign, and failure to stop at a railroad crossing (he had come very close to getting flattened). It was getting extremely difficult to visit Botas Meadas, who lived on the opposite edge of town next to the whorehouse that was located directly across the street from Sheriff Sapo Sánchez.

And now he longed to see Paris again before he went completely crazy, bien loco. Paris—even though the people there had funny accents and the Mexican food tasted like crap. They didn't know how to fix an enchilada, much less an enchilada plate. It was a milagro the people who ate there weren't in wheelchairs. And their tacos? A burro couldn't hold them down. Chiles rellenos? There should be a law against impersonating a mejicano who knew what the hell to do to a chile. It was like knowing how to make love to a woman. You didn't just throw her around then flip her in bed. Slow and smooth—that was the secret. Good cheese, batter stirred slowly, smoothly. One had to put the cheese in slowly. And softly. Then you tasted the results. Slowly. Smoothly. These people didn't know you had to take your time. The only people who could eat that stuff were the turistas. "My, how delicious! My, authentic Mexican food. You certainly couldn't get this back in Iowa!" Wanna bet? Spread it around the house, lady. You won't have rats for a hundred years. Try it on your husband or lover, your mistress. You'll get your wish and the cook will go to the big house—but you won't. Otherwise, a beautiful town. No dogs, no cats, no rats, and everybody's marriage seems secure. Everybody strolls hand in hand. Everything seems slow. And smooth.

And the girl he had met in Paris! Beautiful! He had spent a day there, strolling in the park, holding hands, revealing secrets, letting the day melt itself away, discussing the war, the future, perhaps a future together, until it was time to say good-bye. Only those who have gone off to war know how heartbreaking a farewell can be. He had promised he would come to Paris again when the war was over if he was fortunate enough to live through it. She had placed a gold chain with a cameo around his neck for good luck. It, too, was nestled among his medals and discharge papers. He would take it to Mass with him when he didn't take the picture of the beautiful alemana. Once he had returned home he started drinking, assuring himself the cheap wine would bring the nightmares to an end in a short time. But here he was thirty years or so later, and somehow he had not succeeded in drinking himself to death. ▪

Yeah, once the *Tribune* up in Albuquerque got hold of the story, the bidding would begin. The Martínezes, with help from their Mafia friends, were sure to outbid everybody, and that meant a never-ending supply of Wild Irish Rose. Hell, if the turistas were already lured by The Emporium's huge yellow and red signs announcing CURIOS, GAS, GENUINE TURQUOISE (about as genuine as María Martínez's outrageous melones), and SUPER DELICIOUS MACAROONS (about as delicious as the crap they called Mexican food in Paris. Hell, the only real cookies were the genuine, old-fashioned gingersnaps) about twenty miles outside San Miguel on Highway 85, then imagine how much money the Martínezes stood to make when they painted FAMOUS SIX-TEEN-FOOT in front of their RATTLER signs.

Already he could see María Martínez dipping into the till, emptying it giddily, the large rattlesnake hide now in her possession (after outbidding the governor, the archbishop, several senators, a madam, several museums, etc.), scratching out fives, tens, twenties and fifties, counting and recounting two, three, even four times, her inch-long ruby-red nails flashing as she flipped the last of the bills into Mosco's outstretched, slightly nervous hand (but only slightly—the only thing he feared, had feared since the war, was the inability to buy, steal, or connive an adequate supply of Wild Irish Rose).

She would, of course, also want to buy the rattles, and he would promise to bring them. He would let her sweat. It would be good for her—learn what it was like to want and wait, be at the mercy of somebody the way most of San Miguel had been at the mercy of the Martínezes for years and years.

In truth, he had hated being placed in that predicament at the Farnsworth Arroyo. He thought—no, swore—he was far stronger, beyond temptation. He didn't believe in the crap Father Schmidt had fumed about that morning, but it had started exactly the way he had predicted: your Guardian Angel tugging at you in one direction, the good, and El Diablo with his cuernos and long cola in the opposite, the bad, towards sin and evil. People would probably laugh and think he was preparing to announce, once again, to the town, the county, that he had witnessed still another milagro sent directly from God to tear him away from the bottle forever. And exactly how many Paris enchiladas did he care to eat, especially now that he was rich as a gringo's suegra, but no, it was true—his guardian angel and El Diablo with his cuernos and long cola had wrestled each other for possession of his soul—two out of three falls, just like Bulldog Plechas and the stinking creep who dared oppose him did Saturday night after Saturday night at the Armory up in Albuquerque. But what was a man supposed to do—pretend that the opportunity, which was surely the work of El Diablo, with his cuernos and long cola, had not presented itself? It was so easy for Father Schmidt to say, with much assurance, the assurance of the Martínezes, "Blessed are the poor . . . ," "Blessed are the meek . . ." (and blessed are those poor cabrones in Paris, who belong in hell, and whose fingers, along with their huevos, should be cut off for making Mexican food the turista raved and raved about and recommended to other turistas who would rave, rave, and recommend to other turistas). And blessed are the Martínezes, who have already inherited all of San Miguel, and soon all of San Miguel County, and the day after that even more, and more! And blessed are the Martínezes, for they drop a large check into the collection basket every Sunday without fail, for their name is on the cornerstone of the church, the parish hall, the hospital, the twenty-four-hour emergency clinic, the jail, The Emporium, city hall, the First San Miguel Bank and Trust (trust?—I'd eat a dozen enchiladas in Paris first), the Thunderbird Bar and Grill, the Grand Macaroon Bakery, Willkie's Lumber Yard, Madman Martínez's Car Lot, Willkie's Grand Furniture Store, and on and on. Yes, blessed were the Martínezes. Very blessed. For they inherited the earth and bought the rest. Yes, it was easy for Father Schmidt to say, "Blessed esto y blessed l'otro." It was as easy for him to dip his long, delicate fingers into the collection basket as it was for the Martínezes to drop a large envelope in with a yawn. ■

So there he was at the top of the Farnsworth Arroyo, his Guardian Angel pulling desperately at the right shoulder of his Sunday morning suit jacket, the faded blue jacket he had gotten married in, while El Diablo with his cuernos and long cola and smelling of sulfur was tugging at the other, intent on pulling him all the way down the arroyo, into the path of the giant rattler. The way they were pulling they were going to rip the sleeves right off his favorite—his only—faded blue suit jacket, old, almost as tough as hide, made when they made things to last.

He had simply been on his way home for a breakfast of raw egg followed by a little, just a little, swig of Wild Irish Rose, then a gingersnap or two followed by another swig, but just a small one, of Wild Irish Rose. Gingersnaps—now those were cookies—not like macaroons, that crap María Martínez sold to the turistas down at The Emporium, more than likely the same turistas who had stopped in Paris to enjoy enchiladas made exclusively for the discriminating taste of Americans.

He remembered that the game between the Yankees and the Dodgers would be on in an hour. Dodgers—a perfect name for a team that was gonna spend the entire day dodging hard-hit singles, butcher-shop doubles, sledgehammer triples, jab, jab, right-cross grounders, demolition-derby line drives, hard, merciless curves, crushing homers, more hard-hit crunching homers. Oh, if he had the money and the contacts His Honor the Mayor had, he'd be watching the game at Yankee Stadium instead of having to listen to it on that piece of junk Ted Turner, proprietor of Ted Turner's Radio Sales and Repair Shop, had nerve enough, the huevos, to call a radio. The game would be carried on KWIL, which was named for Willkie, the Martínezes' son, 90.1 on your radio dial. He was just about to turn onto the road that led directly to his house when El Diablo, with his cuernos and long cola, who had tricked his Guardian Angel into thinking he had won, grabbed Mosco from behind (cobarde) and sent him flying over the edge of the Farnsworth Arroyo. Mosco barely had time to take off his glasses and jam the bundle of frayed *Albuquerque Tribune* sports pages securely into the back pocket of his faded, timeworn overalls.

His Guardian Angel got the worst of it as he fought fiercely to keep Mosco from stutter-stepping all the way down the slippery south wall of the arroyo while El Diablo, with his cuernos and long cola, wrapped in a cloud of sulfur, could do nothing but smile as he leaned on Mosco, ever grateful for human weakness and for gravity. ■

And then Father Schmidt asked Mosco if he had been drinking, and Mosco admitted he had. "Sí, but no más un tragito," and then Father Schmidt asked how much was "un tragito," and Mosco said he had stopped at Elio's Gas Station for a bottle of bootleg wine before Mass and had had only a tragito, un poquito, only a little bit, and then only a few tragitos, to save some for dessert with his gingersnaps.

Father Schmidt, as usual, asked, surprised, if Mosco truly ate gingersnaps. Mosco responded, "Yes, Father, I truly do. Those are real cookies, not like that crap María Martínez sells down at The Emporium." "My son! Your language, my son! This is the house of God. Every time you use such language, you are driving a nail deeper into Christ's hand." Mosco apologized, saying he meant no harm to Christ. He was simply getting ready to tell Father Schmidt about "the Greatest Cookies in the World, the most delicious, the most sabrosos, ¡chinga'o!" "My son, my son!" Father Schmidt interrupted, "I, too, am extremely fond of gingersnaps, but more often than not they are a test of my willpower. I could eat an entire bag at one sitting, but with milk, not Wild Irish Rose. Had you acquired a taste for milk and not for wine, you would shame the devil and walk away from temptation every single time, every single time El Dee-a-bolo con sus ku-air-nos and long cola and smelling of esufray tried to tangle with you." "Es verdad, es verdad," Mosco said as fervently as possible.

"He had to admit to himself that at one time or another his drinking had caused everybody in San Miguel some kind of grief through his hallucinations, his countless promises to stop drinking, his . . . He had tried to end his grief and his life with a million—no, two million—tragitos of cheap wine, daring El Diablo con sus ku-air-nos y long cola, and smelling of sulfur, I mean esufray, to take him, but his Guardian Angel had always stood up for him, beating the crap out of his opponents, worthless pieces of . . . uh, the way he made them pay for their sins Saturday night after Saturday night at the Armory up in Albuquerque—"

"My son! My son! My son! You are in the house . . . Oh, my Lord, grant me patience . . . For your penance recite ten rosaries—

no, make that fifteen rosaries—so that your tongue may be tamed, and that it not know the taste of Thunderbird—" "Of Wild Irish Rose, Father. I switched brands." "Of Wild Irish Rose, then, and attend early morning Mass for a month." "¡Chinga'o!" "What was that you said, my son?" "Gingersnaps con leche, Father. From now on it's gingersnaps con leche. The best god . . . the best cookies God ever made, don't you agree, Father?" "Bendito sea Deeos, bendito sea Deeos," Father Schmidt replied, as happy as if he were entering the Kingdom of Heaven, or the doors of The Emporium, hunting for gingersnaps with the same zeal that fueled him when searching for lost souls. María Martínez kept the gingersnaps hidden behind the hundreds of boxes of her WORLD-FAMOUS MACAROONS.

"¡Chinga'o!" Mosco thought. He needed a tragito, some Wild Irish Rose, un poquito, just a little bit. Before long this was going to be worse than spending a day in hell trying, almost crying, desperately trying to get your driver's license as Sheriff Sapo Sánchez grilled you, intimidated you, bullied you, that cabrón pansón, shouting, barking orders, execute a right-hand turn, qué chinga'os era execute a right-hand turn? Yeah, execute, that was what was on your mind the entire day as you drove around San Miguel getting lectured on adjusting your inside mirror, your outside mirror, your posture, how to look left, how to look right, how to open your door, the hood, the trunk, the glove box, in addition to learning the codes for speeding, broken speedometer, expired license, speeding (again, in case you forgot), a loud muffler, a loud radio, honking too loud or too long, shouting too loud at a friend or an animal, an enemy, in addition to learning all the signs: stop, rr, yield, and a thousand other things you forget because you've been sneaking tragitos every chance you get, like when you stepped outside to check the tire pressure, which you do every ten minutes or five miles, whichever comes first, and all the while you've been thinking execute, execute, like do away with coffee breaks so that Sheriff Sapo Sánchez will not be allowed to stop for "an enchilada special with extra guacamole and sour cream, and apple pie (whatever is left after the noon hour), à la mode, two scoops, please, every hour on the dot, hungry, mighty hungry, upholding the law is hard work, demanding work." All you had to do was think of food and you'd easily come up with a way of executing him.

But Mosco wasn't through. No, not yet. He began his real confession by announcing that all of San Miguel was against him. It was no wonder he could never stop drinking. They—and he thought he knew who *they* were, but he wasn't mentioning any names without a lawyer present. If he had learned anything from experience with the sixteen-foot rattler, it was to get a lawyer. It was a treacherous world. A treacherous world. Yeah, he thought he knew who *they* were. He suspected they met at night at the mayor's house, or at Sheriff Sapo Sánchez's in his cellar, or possibly even in Caruso's Garage to plot how to get him to drink, to cheat and lie and steal and then cheat and lie and steal some more, and then get even—punish him by chaining one arm to a bed (in the mayor's guest house?) and the other to María Martínez and let her play with his chorizo while she rammed one box of macaroons after another down his throat until the sun came up.

"My son! My son! My son! This is the house of God! The house of God! These impure thoughts, they are the work of the devil (con sus cuernos y long cola and smelling of esufray)! The Evil One walks amongst us! An act of confession! Oh, pray, Mr. Zamora, pray fervently, for the Evil One is amongst us!"

"Puro pedo," Mosco thought. He suggested to Father Schmidt that a foolproof way to beat the crap out of the Evil One was to bring in a lawyer. That would cure him of walking amongst us. "Oh, Father, I have to confess. I went to Paris, first class all the way, and now they're after me, and I'm up to my ass with lawyers."

"My son! My son! My . . ." ▪

At his office at the University of New Mexico, Professor of Anthropology Frank Finch Farnsworth clunked the phone down, done with Payroll, relieved to be completing the last stage of his plans to become Professor Emeritus. He kicked both legs up on his old desk that for the first time in thirty years was free of maps, pottery shards, wooden masks, spear points, fossils, a prized photo of

Richard Nixon receiving an award from Ike, the governor and the Martínezes on either side, and pile upon pile of research papers authored by him that had been published in the most prominent anthropology journals the world over. His walls were free of price-less Navajo rugs, zebra hide, snake hides from every corner of the globe, photo after photo posed with Richard Nixon, a large spear point, and a map of Farnsworth Arroyo (where he had uncovered evidence of early man in New Mexico), photos of him with Rocky Marciano, Humphrey Bogart, Maurice Chevalier, and many others. The kachina dolls, shrunken heads, clay pots, baskets, and other mementos from the many times he had circled the globe had been trucked down to his new home in San Miguel. He had one more load or so, and all these mementos would be nestled in their new home.

Earlier that morning the maintenance men had carted off the last of the overstuffed boxes full of hundreds of pages of class notes, field notes written among the hill people in Laos, Burma, Indochina, Thailand, the Philippines, Cambodia, among the peoples of Africa, South America, Central America, and Mexico, along with corre-spondence that was to be housed at the Farnsworth Museum in San Miguel (financed by the Honorable Raymundo Martínez and his wife María and with their son Willkie), and, of course, the notes for his best-selling book, *Early Man in New Mexico*, used for many many years as a class text. If Professor Farnsworth wasn't a millionaire, he was certainly very close. He still had to decide which of his thou-sands of books to keep and which to part with. Already he had taken, um, say two, three loads down to San Miguel but had ended up donating most of them to the Willkie Martínez Library (branch libraries for Los Brasos, Las Animas, Los Chávez, Gallinas, and La Plata were still in the planning stage). The rest he had thrown away. Whatever wasn't fit for the archives at the university or the Willkie Martínez Library was certainly not fit for his home. All that was left was to turn in his grades and drive south to his new home. The acreage he had purchased was, um, just a half mile or so east of San Miguel, where he had discovered the Farnsworth Point, evidence of the oldest form of human life in New Mexico.

One of his most prized, cherished moments was when Richard Nixon came to San Miguel to congratulate him. A valuable discovery. He had advanced the hopes of mankind, blazed a trail that our youth were sure to follow, selflessly given of his time so that the world could profit from his efforts, promoted the cause for ethics—for high standards in the university demonstrated to the world that America was among the leaders in research, demonstrated what dogged persistence and a little Yankee ingenuity could do, what good citizenship could produce. "Therefore, in conjunction with the governor (and the Martínezes) he was declaring this day, December 7, 1953, a day of triumph and not Japanese chicanery, triumph of the American spirit. Let it be known that today, all over the state of New Mexico, this day be known as Professor Frank Finch Farnsworth Day!"

Now all there was to do was to drive to The Emporium, um, two, three times a week for a box of María Martínez's world-famous, delicious, mouth-watering, scrumptious, heartwarming, never-stay-long-on-the-shelf, keep-coming-back-for-more, more, the Pride of America—according to Richard Nixon—macaroons, the only snacks between bouts at the typewriter, start cranking out what was sure to be a long list of best-sellers: a series of detective novels with a Navajo policeman as the main character who uses Navajo philosophy and psychology along with the traditional thinking of the belaganaa, the white man, to bring criminals from the four corners of the reservation to justice.

He had enough knowledge of Navajo culture and had been reading detective novels and magazines for the last, um, fifteen, twenty years, and he also knew the reservation well, having been made a consultant to the Dinéh by Dennis Roanhorse, the tribal chairman. Both medals had been blessed by a medicine man named Hosteen Nakai and placed around his neck by the Honorable Raymundo Martínez and María Martínez, who claimed to be part Navajo (but only in private or perhaps when politically expedient). There were stories in her family about the marauding Navajos who had taken two young boys captive as slaves, and how, um, years later one of the boys returned with his Navajo wife. The children the woman bore were the great-grandparents of María Martínez. The entire town knew this story, but María Martínez had always pretended this business of Navajos and slaves and children had absolutely nothing to do with her. If she admitted these facts to be true (to Chairman Roanhorse, for instance), she did so only in private. She did a lot of business with weavers and silversmiths (she offered quality goods besides the tin concha belts and fake turquoise) in general, and the tribe in particular. It seemed that secretly, slyly, she was learning the language from those who wove and who hammered silver. It was hard to tell just how much cash she paid for the goods because she paid in rolls held together by rubber bands. Her business trips to the reservation offered her an opportunity to, um, learn the customs that had been a way of life long before the abduction of the two little boys. And the fact that she had dressed in a velveteen blouse and skirt with a squash-blossom necklace when she placed the medal honoring him as Friend of the Dinéh around his neck seemed somehow to authenticate that she, in her own manner, was celebrating the very stories she had denied. Yes, he had been twice decorated by the Dinéh. He knew them, and they knew him. They had been friends for years and would remain friends for years to come. And yes, yes, he knew the reservation quite well, thank you. So who better equipped to churn out, um, two, three suspense-filled, wholesome, culturally authentic, patriotic, unpretentious novels a year? And with a blurb by Dick Nixon? "Superb! Simply superb!"   ■

A couple of days after he had battled for his life at the bottom of the Farnsworth Arroyo, Mosco told *The Albuquerque Tribune* only a fraction of the story. He had had to shred his neckerchief and stuff piece after piece into his ears. Otherwise, he would've lost his hearing, the BZZZZZZ of the rattles was so shrill (hell, that wasn't the word he used. What the hell was wrong with *loud?*) . . .   ■

Oh, it certainly wasn't easy being the mayor's wife: having to be responsible for the mayor's social calendar, the macaroons, The Emporium's hired help, serving as the chairwoman of the San

Miguel County Republican Party, offering political advice to her husband (for which she never, never charged the town, not one single cent), and, on top of all that, she still had to deal with people all the damned day long, walking in, trying to unload one scheme after another on her. People like Facundo García, for example, trying to sell the rights to the lawn mower he had converted into a piñón-picking machine. A brilliant idea, but impractical. Day after day, people trying to take advantage of her. Day after day after day. No, it was just not easy being married to the mayor. She had to remind herself constantly that her social standing demanded that she be courteous, act like a lady in front of her customers.

To be courteous, always, especially with Mosco Zamora, a rascal, a liar, a conniver, a drunk two times over, a lawbreaker, an ingrate, a sinner, a skunk, a natural-born wino, but at least ten times as smart as anybody in the Republican Party, but not as smart as her husband. What could Mr. Zamora have for her today? She had to admit he always presented an interesting challenge, that more often than not he made her day.

"Buenos días, le dé Dios, Señora Martínez. ¿Cómo está usted?"

"Muy bien, gracias, señor Zamora, y usted?"

"Bien, bien. And his honor the mayor, ¿cómo sigue?"

"Pues bien. Busy—busy as ever. Busy, busy!"

"¿Y el Willkie? I bet he's got straight A's."

"También bien. I'm proud—so proud of him. He'll be graduating from UNM in a few days. A degree in political science with a minor in accounting. He will follow in his father's footsteps. His father, too, is very, very proud of him. He belonged to a prestigious fraternity. We're sending him to Paris for a well-deserved vacation before he goes to work as an advisor to the Town of San Miguel."

"Ah, Paris! A lovely place in springtime!"

"Sí, es cierto. I'm sure my Willkie will enjoy it. He took a French class to prepare himself. The girls, you know. We're trying to convince him to run when his father steps down. He's every bit as smart as his father, you know. We need to continue to implement our progressive ideas: new libraries, new roads, lower taxes, better schools throughout San Miguel County. San Miguel needs a leader like Willkie. But everything in its own good time, I always say. Oh, yes—speaking of time, I need to serve as hostess for a tea to raise funds to keep my Raymundo in office. As you know, I'm the chairwoman of the San Miguel County Republican Party, a position that demands a lot of my time. So how may I be of service today, Mr. Zamora? You never fail to come in with such wonderful and challenging ideas and approaches to life. In another life you would have been Euclid or Newton. Yes, Newton more than Euclid. Newton, the most wonderful of thinkers. As far as I'm concerned, the world will never see a genius like him again."

"Well, I know you're an extremely busy woman (la mera mera de esos cabrones Republicanos) so I'll get to the point. Yesterday, on my way home from Mass, I came across a víbora at the bottom of the Farnsworth Arroyo. Not just a víbora but, well—let me put it this way: if I was to charge you and His Honor the Mayor by the square inch for the hide . . ."

The Albuquerque Tribune
May 2, 1974
GIANT RATTLER FOUND IN SAN MIGUEL!
Martín Zamora yanked off his glasses and wiped them quickly on the lapel of his suit jacket in order to confirm what he had seen winding its way across the bottom of the Farnsworth Arroyo: the largest víbora he had ever seen.

Please see RATTLER, A–2

The Albuquerque Tribune
May 4, 1974
WORLDWIDE FAME FOR M. ZAMORA!
Mr. Martín Zamora of San Miguel, New Mexico, the man who discovered the 16-foot rattler at the bottom of the Farnsworth Arroyo only half a mile or so east of that central New Mexican town, is now known the whole world over. Pictures of him holding the hide of

that giant víbora have appeared all over Europe, Asia, Africa, Latin America, and anywhere a newspaper is printed. There are confirmed reports that his picture appeared in a one-page newspaper on a small island in the South Pacific. In Paris, *Le Monde*

Please see ZAMORA, A–2

The Albuquerque Tribune
May 11, 1974
QUESTIONS ABOUT GIANT RATTLER

The authenticity of the giant víbora found near Farnsworth Arroyo was called into question yesterday when Billy Bob Harris, a herpetologist from Paris, Texas, home of the famous "Rattlesnake Roundup," reported that the patterns on the hide seemed to indicate that the world-famous "víbora" may not be a rattler after all. In addition, Mr. Harris stated that the extremely brittle condition of the hide seemed to indicate that it was much older than the "víbora" Mr. Martin Zamora claimed to have discovered winding its way down the bottom of the Farnsworth Arroyo.

Please see RATTLER, A–2

The San Miguel Tribune
May 18, 1974
FAMED ANTHROPOLOGIST TO INSPECT "RATTLER" TODAY

Famed anthropologist Dr. Frank Finch Farnsworth, eminent world traveler, distinguished educator, explorer, author, philanthropist, patriot, citizen of the world, and friend of San Miguel, will meet today with the mayor of San Miguel, the Honorable Raymundo Martínez, and his wife, María Martínez, chairwoman of the San Miguel County Republican Party, in an effort to verify the authenticity of the 16-foot "víbora" found recently by San Miguel native Martín Zamora near the site where Dr. Farnsworth discovered a spear point that put to rest all theories that New Mexico man had migrated from Texas. Dr. Farnsworth proved without a doubt that the New Mexico man had been living in what is now "The Land of Enchantment" for at least two hundred thousand to four hundred thousand years before the invasion of what today are known as tejanos, our neighbors, who continue to cling to the theory that this land is theirs to plunder in the name of tourism today as it was four hundred thousand years ago.

Dr. Farnsworth, who has traveled all over the world, is recognized by his peers as an expert in identifying a wide range of snakes from all over the globe: the mutant, the exotic, the Machiavellian, the recluse, the psychotic, the territorial, the loner, the narcissist, the ostracized, the wide variety of colors, skin patterns, predictable and unpredictable behavior, and, of course, the effect caused by the arrival of man, his machinery, the noise, the fear, and the confusion, all of which manifest themselves in change of pigmentation, ferocity, and methods of attack, according to Dr. Farnsworth. Dr. Farnsworth will also advise His Honor the Mayor and his wife about the possibility of his traveling to Washington in a last-minute attempt to persuade key officials, among whom it is rumored is the president, to convince the chairmen of the Finance and Defense Committees to allocate approximately one hundred thousand dollars of disaster relief funds to help defray the cost incurred by the Town of San Miguel for purchasing the hide of the giant víbora that turned out to be a disastrous fake. The hide was purchased with funds from the town's Kindergarten Development Fund. Mrs. Martínez stated that originally the purpose of purchasing the hide was to donate it to the Willkie Martínez Library, where it was to be placed on permanent display as a state as well as a natural treasure.

Please see RATTLER, A–2

ON THIS DAY IN HISTORY

The following May 18, 1954 article is reproduced to commemorate the 20th anniversary of a pivotal event precipitating the Vietnam War.

DIEN BIEN PHU FALLS TO COMMUNISTS

The brutal 55-day siege of Dien Bien Phu is over. French resistance collapsed as the Communists slogged through mud, overran their trenches, and captured their airfield. The French lost 4,000 men. They killed 8,000 Viet Minh. Word of the collapse came in a radio report from Gen. Christian de Castries: "After 20 hours of fighting without respite, including hand-to-hand combat, the enemy has infiltrated the whole center. We lack ammunition. The Viet Minh are now within a few meters from the radio transmitter from where I am speaking." A few moments later the radio went dead.

Please see HISTORY, A–2

The doctor was tall, with big hands, broad shoulders, iron jaw, long arms and legs—strong enough maybe to hit five homers like Stan Musial had in a 1954 doubleheader, setting a major-league record.

You could see little red viboritas. Crawling all over his face, like the ones on high-class winos in the movies or like on the pendejos who met with the mayor at The Emporium for breakfast every morning. And the doctor talked exactly like the captain who had questioned him about going to Paris: long sentences, big words, long pauses. And he had a lot of hair. White, like the guy in the castle who experimented with body parts until he created a human. Human but a monster. Pobrecito. He wanted to know what the arroyo that was named after him was called in Spanish, so I told him. He repeated it two, three times to himself, and then he asked what it meant in English, and I told him, and then he turned even redder than chile pequín. ▪

"So he claims he killed it, um, two, three weeks ago, maybe longer, and promises to bring in the rattles in two, um, three days so we can examine them? No need for that, María— no need."

"Why's that, Frank?"

"There aren't any."

"Not any? There damn well better be some, Frank. I mean it. This is my town and nobody—not even the Chicago people up in Albuquerque—better try to pull that kind of bullshit on María Martínez. You tell me why there aren't any while I clean my trusty revolver. I'm doing this job myself. I don't need to sic the hired help on some slimy jerk who tried to take advantage of a lady—"

"Well, um, first of all, the extreme desiccated condition of the hide leads me to believe that it has been dead much longer than Mr. Zamora claims. And second, it's not a *Crotalus atrox*."

"Get to the point, Frank."

"Well, it's a python . . . a *Python reticulatus*."

"A fraud, Frank? That conniving, lying, good-for-nothing, natural-born wino pulled—"

"I realized it immediately. Now calm down, calm down. I'll tell you how. I wanted to break it to you gently, and I just didn't know how. The truth of the matter is that it was mine to begin with. I bagged it years ago in southwest Indochina. It graced the wall of my office, where students and faculty alike would marvel at its beauty and size. Senators, actresses, directors, writers, visiting diplomats, war heroes, famed singers and chanteuses, Charlie Chaplin, Marlene, and many others had their pictures taken with that hide. A lot of fond memories, María, a lot of very fond memories. It hurt me when it came time to part with it, but it had lost its beauty. For everything there is a season, María. So I very unceremoniously threw it out with whatever else deserved to be called junk when I first moved down here."

"Oh Frank, Frank, where exactly did you . . . ?"

"I just learned it, the Spanish name for the Farnsworth Arroyo: El Dompay Viejo."

"¿El Dompe Viejo? Oh, no, no, Frank, no. That lying, conniving . . .

"A fraud, Frank! A fraud! Big people—Chicago people up in Albuquerque with their contribution, we were able to convince the president of the museum to buy the hide for the permanent collection. We had it sold for—how should I say it—a handsome sum. But someone tipped off Chicago, and the next thing you know a representative of the museum comes in with some hick herpetologist from Texas, and the whole venture is blown to hell. All we would've had to do is print a story in the *Tribune* explaining to the town that the mayor had been forced to sell the hide to restore some funds into the depleted town treasury, get the Chicago Museum to cut us an official check for half the bill and hand over the other half in cash, and heigh-ho Silver, away! That's why Ray had to talk to you about inspecting the hide—it would give us some credibility, respectability. If we were calling for an inspection ourselves, then we were definitely not part of the hoax, you see? You'll be adequately compensated in due time, Frank. In due time. Ray and I are okay with the Chicago people, Frank, but we owe them. They're gonna want their money sooner or later. If they don't get it tomorrow, or the day after, or the day after that, they won't mind—the interest will double every week, and the week after, and the week after that. Eventually, if you don't pay, you die so dead nobody will ever find you.

"So it appears we were fleeced, and fleeced by the best. They threw in what we asked. They set the interest rate, which was high, but what did we care? We were gonna strike, get the money, and pay them back much sooner than later. But the museum director was their man in Chicago. He played us like we were small-town hicks, Frank. We never saw it coming, then the Chicago folks brought the herpetologist in with as much publicity as possible. We were dead meat, jerky, carne seca. We owned a giant snake hide that was worthless, and we had a pile of IOUs in the safe that we owed interest on—a lot of interest. What those Chicago gentlemen forget is that they are living in our state, and sooner or later the Good Fairy's gonna visit them. We know senators, the governor, and a lot of other people who can make life miserable for them. We're gonna squeeze them slowly, so slowly.

They are going to pay, Frank, and I want to start with returning their money—see the look on their faces when I drop the sacks on the table. And announce it's all there, their benevolent loan plus the interest.

"You have got to go to Washington, Frank. With your connections, we'll get some development money, and then I'm gonna go after those bastards. They think they took María Martínez on a train ride past the bank and down the hole of her abandoned outhouse without knowing a thing. I hope they keep on thinking that. I'm calling out the dogs, Frank—and by the way, your wino friend is gonna pay, too. Mr. Martín Zamora, conniver, schemer, con artist, smooth talker, natural-born wino, the biggest burr under the saddle of San Miguel, un Diablo bien hecho, thief, ladrón, underhanded son of a . . . oh, hell, yes—he'll pay. He's gonna return the money I laid out for that hide. Hide? I'll take it out of his hide! I'll do it with lawyers, so the town can see how reasonable I can be. I'll put a request out, Frank. Any bar that sells him one drop of alcohol loses its license. He'll regret the day he saw that hide down at the bottom of the Farnsworth Arroyo and saw dollar bills raining from the sky. *My* dollar bills, Frank. And if I have to pay interest, so does he. I hope he enjoys Paris, because I'm gonna own him the rest of his godforsaken life." ▪

Sheriff Sapo Sánchez had the siren wailing all the way to the Albuquerque airport, where he arrived, warrant in hand, only minutes before the departure of TWA flight 1974, bound for Paris. The young man with the reddish crew cut and twisted smile checked the flight roster but was unable to find a Mr. Martín Zamora listed. Sheriff Sapo Sánchez was sure that the suspect had boarded under an assumed name and insisted the flight be delayed until such time as the suspect was apprehended. He waved the warrant frantically in the young man's face, threatening to arrest him for conspiracy—for aiding and abetting a known criminal, a blackmailer, an extortionist. ▪

"Whadda ya mean, Frank? Of course he went to Paris!"

"Yes, María, he did."

"Okay, then. The little weasel thinks he walked into The Emporium and walked out with every single box of macaroons and a wheelbarrow full of silver dollars."

"But not to the Paris you're thinking about."

"Not to the Paris I'm thinking about? Okay, Frank. Get to the point—get to the point. This entire affair has cost me a lot of money, and I would've had to part with The Emporium if it hadn't been for your influence, Frank. It almost cost Ray his job and his political future. He blamed me for throwing in with the Chicago boys, but he wasn't against it when I first came up with the idea. It's caused some bitter feelings on both sides. Bitter feelings. I have to come up with some money to get him to smile again. And I want to see him smile again. I want him to run for governor and then for senator. But right now I have to get this business of Mr. Martín Zamora cleared up. So you say he didn't go to the Paris I was thinking about? What exactly do you mean, Frank?"

"Well, um, first of all I need to tell you I had a strange feeling, very strange feeling, since the very beginning of this business of Mr. Martín Zamora and the sixteen-foot rattler. Of course I was quite busy, carting down as much stuff from my office and garage as I possibly could, along with going through the tortures, of, um, retirement.

"Nevertheless, I managed to get through to a friend in Washington—a friend who, you might say, keeps the, um, darkest secrets of men. He has kept track of domestic enemies—well, let's tell the truth, of commies—for a quarter of a century or more. He knows all the names and all the places, as well as the times. And one of the names in his—you might say—private archives, is a Mr. Martín Zamora, who stepped off a troop train and, instead of reboarding, got on a train that would eventually come to a stop in Paris. According to the report, Mr. Zamora, upon stepping off, headed directly to the Mexican café as if he had been expertly briefed by agents sympathetic to establishing Communism as a way of life right here in America, the land of the free and the home of the brave, home of the Liberty Bell, of Old Glory, of Richard Nixon—um, in short, of everything that stands for good in the world, especially for those downtrodden countries that have been enslaved by the tyranny of the hammer and sickle. Reportedly, Mr. Zamora exchanged the universal secret signal with the cook, a Gabriel Sánchez, who was the hayfay, or kingpin, for that particular province. The two members of that nefarious group of shameless, unpatriotic bloodsuckers then got to work. Remember that their mission was to exchange and then take back to their spineless leaders—who would gladly burn the American flag in public if they could skirt a law or two—information that would be examined in order to, um, determine a plan of action that would lead best to cutting out the heart of America and *then* eating it for good measure. What they came up with was quite simple but very clever and effective. Mr. Zamora would order a plate, eat a little, then pretend to be totally appalled by the taste and proceed to eat something else. Again he would become angered, and the cook would come and take his plate away and return with a new order. It became evident to our agent that they were passing messages back and forth. The cook would pull the cryptic message out of a taco or a chile relleno or from under some enchiladas. Later, the cook's way of delivering his messages was to bring out a plate counter to what Mr. Zamora had asked for. For example, if Mr. Zamora asked for a taco, the cook would come out of the kitchen with an enchilada. The significance of each food item, ordered and supposedly mistakenly brought to the table, remains classified and will remain so until the year, um, 2015. Thus were the venomous messages exchanged, then later delivered to one chief and another until it reached the party leaders, those cockroaches that live in the dark but who send others out into the world to do their work for them—work that by necessity must be carried out in the light of day.

"Well, a lot of people would deny the fact that Mr. Zamora was and is a commie simply on the basis of a psychiatric report written after his secret mission to Paris, when he had been questioned and then escorted by two MPs to the commie sympathizer in charge of determining the mental status of people such as Mr. Zamora, who not only was suspected of belonging to the party and performing, um, nefarious tasks in the name of Karl Marx, but was also a soldier who had gone AWOL in a time of war.

"Mr. Zamora, of course, never knew about the report filed by the captain, in which he was neither charged nor cleared. However, it can be noted that the word *treason* appears one hundred and sixteen times in the report and the words *suspected member and espionage agent* appear one hundred and twelve times. Thus was a noose placed around the neck of one Mr. Martín Zamora. Now, many would argue that it would have been extremely difficult to prove the secret mission, the Mexican restaurant scenario, in a military court. I think otherwise. The evidence was there. An agent witnessed the exchange of information—information that might have helped swing the war in favor of those atheist bastards who fling innocent babies into the air and then let them land on the bayonets of their bloodthirsty rifles. Mr. Zamora managed to save his neck because he had returned to his unit of his own free will. Well, that was the ruling of the psychiatrist, who stated that Mr. Zamora should be allowed to stay in uniform because not one shred of evidence proving he was a commie son of a you-know-what could be produced.

"What the psychiatrist didn't know was that the captain had filed an additional report stating that Mr. Zamora was a security risk and, though not under full surveillance, would be watched throughout his time in uniform and placed under complete surveillance the minute he discarded his uniform and became an ordinary civilian again. By the way, his commanding officers were given the okay from on high to award Mr. Zamora his medals due to the fact that he had distinguished himself tremendously on the field of battle and, just as importantly, had not committed any act that could be defined as, um, treason. Or at least had not been seen or had not been caught committing such an act. More than likely, he could not have had much time to commit treason if he was constantly dodging bullets. The real proof would come when he returned home to the boiling cauldron of the espionage wars, the war to win the hearts and minds not only of his country, but of smaller countries we would have to save from the jaws of the tiger. He would also be awarded the smallest amount of money possible when it came to his disability check, though it is not noted in his records, as a form of retribution for his disloyalty as well as to assure that he could never afford to travel more than two or three hundred miles from his residence. If he happened to venture beyond that, our agents would know he had been sent some money and was off on a mission for the Great Satan. This would also allow the, um, company to free up one of the two agents shadowing him and, thus, add one more knight to the valiant struggle raging across our land with the fury of an unchecked, voracious disease for which there is no cure.

"Now for the psychiatric nonsense. According to the report, Mr. Zamora had begun experiencing a bizarre and horrible dream a year prior to his induction. 'He didn't know it then, but he had foreseen his future,' notes the good doctor, a commie who had infiltrated the army in order to keep as many of our boys as possible from honoring their oath, their word—encouraging them to go and stay AWOL. I can see Mr. Zamora flinging one cow pie after another, along with some genuine New Mexico bull crap, at this man, who had flashed the international, secret sign the minute he walked into the room.

"To continue: What had Mr. Zamora claimed he had seen in his dream? Well, it was a man—a man barely visible because of a strong, violent rain that had been falling, it seems, for two weeks and more, making his way to the top of the muddy, slippery hill towards Mr. Zamora, both arms outstretched as if ready to welcome Mr. Zamora with a strong abrazo. In his left hand he held a medal—for valor, perhaps—and in his right hand he wielded the sharpest of bayonets. It was evident now that the man was a soldier wearing the uniform of a specially trained brigade named 'Der Führer's Dobermans.' As he came closer it became—to repeat myself—evident that his head had been lopped off with a blunt saw. The psychiatrist had nothing but sympathy for Mr. Zamora and, predictably, recommended that he be, um, transferred out of the infantry to another military occupation such as cook or radio dispatcher in the Signal Corps. His recommendation was, of course, rightfully turned down.

"Of special interest in Mr. Zamora's file are some orders recommending him for a Silver Star for his bravery on a hill near Paris where he had, in hand-to-hand combat, distinguished himself by taking control of his platoon when the sergeant in charge fell victim to a bayonet thrust repeatedly into his stomach and throat, thus helping to repel a charge by the unit known as 'Der Führer's Dobermans,' who had a well-earned reputation for their fury and failure to surrender. Mr. Zamora's orders for a Silver Star were downgraded to a Bronze Star." ▪

Hell, if María Martínez called Senator Chávez, he'd contact Senator Chávez, too. And if María Martínez wanted to sic her Mafia lawyers on him, he'd buy himself some lawyers, too. Mean lawyers such as Fito Quintana, full of barbed wire and capable of being crazy as locoweed and yerba mala too, chinga'o. Seguro que hell yes! What the hell. He had tangled with El Diablo, with his cuernos and long cola and smelling of esufray, and lived to tell the tale, and he had drained four thousand, three hundred bottles of cheap tokay and that hadn't killed him. And he had cut off a young soldier's head with an entrenching tool and had nearly lost his head in return, and only now that he was losing his memory did he care to take, finally, a good look at his life and attempt to accept the past with all its horrors, with all the beauty that had passed him by, no matter whose fault it was, and simply learn to appreciate everything. What the hell. He had at last been given a chance to live, to love, and, yes, even to die. There were many, many who were killed by bullets, artillery, and, yes, bayonets and entrenching tools. It was late but perhaps not too late. He had to live for them.

It was springtime, and he had a round-trip ticket to Paris. And what the hell, he was going first class, all the way.

La Promesa

At the time of this story, there were rumors flying all over the county about El Hombre sin Cabeza, the headless man. He had been seen (it seems he appeared only at night) just this side of Las Animas, then near the dirt road that winds west from Gallinas to Todos Zamoras. Caruso Zamora, who Saturday night after Saturday night won the demolition derby and who had been issued more traffic citations than anybody else in the entire county, had seen him as he was flying down the highway in his tow truck somewhere between Gallinas and Los Brasos, and when he saw him he floored the accelerator and zoomed right by Sheriff Sánchez's speed trap at well over a hundred miles an hour and kept it floored all the way to San Miguel, where Sapo wrote out citations for "espeeding, a violation of Civil Code Two Twenty-Nine Point One; for hazardous driving, a Two Fourteen Point Three; for failure to yield the right of way, a Two Twenty Point Ten; for failure to stop at a posted sign, a Two Seventeen Point Eleven; for running through a barrier at a railroad crossing, a Two Twelve Point Three Zero; for driving the wrong way on a one-way street . . ."

Many had seen El Hombre sin Cabeza in the cemetery outside San Miguel on his hands and knees, desperately clawing at the ground as if attempting to unearth a coffin. In every story he had shredded, bleeding fingers, and his pants were frayed, tattered, and soaked with blood at the knees.

But it was Mosco Zamora, the famous Mosco who years back was in the newspaper statewide, nationwide, as well as worldwide for two weeks, photo after photo of him with that sixteen-foot rattler he had found inching its way down the bottom of the

Farnsworth Arroyo. Yes, it was Mosco who had first seen El Hombre sin Cabeza—coincidentally, in Farnsworth Arroyo—one moonless night when the headless one came walking towards him, arms outspread, shouting "¡Mosco! ¡Mosco! ¡Mosco!"

But enough of El Hombre sin Cabeza. For now.

This story really begins the morning Mosco, who had begun seeing moscas dive-bombing at him a week or so before, broke the window of The Emporium, not even realizing that he, a drunk for most of the twenty-nine years since the war, had been chosen by God as a vehicle for a milagro—a milagro far more authentic than when he had claimed he had seen a burning rosary on his bedroom wall and had given up drinking—for three or four days or so.

Later that day, when Mosco learned about the milagro, he not only made a promesa to stop drinking (NO MORE THUNDER-BIRD! FOREVER!) but also announced that he would make a pilgrimage to the old church across more than a mile of llano—no, not on foot, but to prove that this time he intended to keep his promesa, on his knees (if somebody could convince his sons, José, Felipe, and Roberto, to accompany him).

At about ten that particular morning, Mosco (at first the moscas were only buzz sounds, buzz—más o menos an arm's length away—buzz buzz) grabbed a tin of buttery macaroons that María Martínez had placed on the table outside The Emporium's front door and flung it against the window. Then, before long, the sounds were accompanied by moscas, only two or three and then suddenly there were squadrons—huge eyes, furry legs, buzz buzz. The tin hit the very spot where one of Sheriff Sapo's stray bullets had hit only an hour or so before. At mosca squadrons, you throw whatever you can find, causing the weblike pattern to expand, and so you break a window and they threaten you first with jail and then with the mayor's Mafia friends.

Had María Martínez known Mosco had just set the workings of a milagro in motion, she wouldn't have run out from behind the counter shrieking, "My macaroons! My macaroons!" threatening Mosco with jail (but wait a minute, that meant calling that idiota Sapo Sánchez, who had just put a hole in the window trying to stop Esteban Zamora, who had just held up the bank. Oh, thank God, ¡Gracias a Dios! that Caruso happened to pass by just then on his way for parts, y ¡Gracias a Dios! que Caruso had rammed Esteban's Dodge all to hell with his tow truck, putting a quick and sure end to his getaway! No, it was useless to call Sapo, that big pendejo. Say—maybe Caruso should run for the sheriff. As chairwoman of the county Republican party she could certainly . . .).

Yes, if María Martínez had known Mosco was responsible for a milagro, she certainly wouldn't have bounced one, two, three tins of macaroons off his thick skull. But how could she have possibly known? After all, it wasn't until around three that very afternoon, when the sun's rays hit the window, that María Martínez saw the face of Jesus on the wall, in the very spot where Esteban Zamora's WANTED poster detailing the bank robberies, stolen cars, fraud, and bigamy had been before his capture, right between the WANTED posters of the two biggest thieves in San Miguel County, the Sánchez brothers, Tranquilino (who, like Esteban, robbed banks) and Salvador (who worked for the IRS).

Later that day, Father Schmidt (who was destined to suffer through milagros such as Mosco's burning rosary and La La La Chevalier's tortilla scorched with the likeness of her dearly departed Lukie) is praying rosary after rosary in front of The Emporium and Sapo is going crazy issuing ticket after ticket (driving the wrong way on a one-way street, that's a Two Nine-Nine Point Seven-Seven; illegal parking, that's a Two Eleven Point Nine-Seven). And María Martínez is smiling and offering three boxes of her famous macaroons and the key to the town to Mosco as he walks through the crowd (como el Charlton Heston parting the Red Sea) into The Emporium as the sun is going down.

Mosco sees the face of Jesus on the wall and hears Jesus say, "Ven m'hijo, buzz buzz."

As the sun sets Mosco announces his promesa to give up drinking (perhaps, he tells himself, he has been responsible for other milagros throughout San Miguel. Earlier that day he had heaved a brick through the front window of La Golondrina and an empty

bottle into the windshield of a classic Thunderbird down at Madman Martínez's Car Lot), inspiring him not only to make a pilgrimage across the wide llano, but to make it on his knees. ▪

The pilgrimage began like this: José, the oldest son (who owned
a cherry-red T-Bird with porthole windows, chrome rims, and
etc.) said, "What, again? No, no, no, no, no!"

Juanita, his wife, who had been at The Emporium when María
Martínez saw the face of Jesus on the wall, pleaded, "But he's
responsible for a milagro. He needs you . . ."

"No, no, no, no, no!"

Then she tried convincing José that Mosco was perhaps a saint,
to which José shook his head quietly, unconvinced. Juanita
reminded him that the only little favor he had to do was pick up
his father at the old church at midnight, after Mosco had completed his pilgrimage.

"In my T-Bird? No, no, no, no, no!" José shrieked, thinking of
the clouds of dust settling on the paint job even if he drove slowly,
slowly across the llano. And the dirt he'd have to vacuum off the
carpet. "No, no, no, no, no!" And who—who was going to help
him wash and wax it when it was all over?

And what about the old bridge. It sagged so badly in the middle it might give way any minute. At any minute.

"The transmission, Juanita, the transmission!" José explained,
holding his hands together to show her how the T-Bird could not
negotiate the tight V of the old bridge. "No, no, no, no, no!"

"Sí, sí, sí, sí, sí," Juanita said. "En tu T-Bird." ▪

Felipe (who was the second oldest son and didn't own a vintage
cherry-red T-Bird with porthole windows, chrome rims, and etc.,
and was, therefore, more tolerant, but not so tolerant that "No,
no, no, not again!" didn't fail to escape from his lips) drove down
to The Emporium immediately (in his Pontiac, after picking up
Roberto) and parted the crowd easily (como el Charlton Heston)
with Roberto immediately behind him, and when Mosco (buzz

buzz "¡Chingadas moscas! No more THUNDERBIRD forever!") saw him, he held out both arms like a martyr of old, ready to take the first "step" of his bloody pilgrimage.

Roberto—who owned a Ford pickup, and because he was the youngest son had very little say in the matter—said patiently, "That's the third time this year he's announced in public he's never going to drink again! Last time he swore he was never going to touch another drop of Thunderbird."

Well, you can imagine how the pilgrimage went if by the end of the first block Mosco's khakis were torn to shreds, his knees scraped and bleeding. He tried to swat away horde after horde of moscas. Felipe and Roberto fought desperately to keep hold of his arms in order to help him along by lifting him with each painful step.

Once they turned the corner of First and Martínez—where the large clock on the front of the First National Bank, owned by the Mafia connection María Martínez had threatened to sic on Mosco, read eight o'clock—there was nothing but the railroad tracks and a mile or so of llano to the church, where José would be waiting impatiently at midnight.

By nine o'clock they had covered about a quarter of a mile after pausing time and again for Mosco to swat away moscas, to gather up courage to continue, his knees torn by the rocks, cactus ("Moscas! NO more Thunderbird! Forever!"), as Felipe and Roberto struggled to keep him on course.

By ten o'clock Mosco had covered half a mile only because Felipe and Roberto had lifted and carried, lifted and carried him with each step he attempted across the moonless llano.

Eleven o'clock. One mile (más o menos).

Eleven thirty. Mosco claimed he saw the church steeple, refused any further help, insisted Felipe and Roberto walk behind him.

Midnight. Mosco stands up, yells he has seen the light. "Never again another drop . . . ," and begins running in the direction of the rays God has sent down especially for him, two golden rays that will guide him directly to the Kingdom of Heaven. Truly, today has been a day of milagros! Truly a day of milagros! He has been forgiven! All that is necessary now is to cross the bridge that spans heaven and earth.

José eases the cherry-red T-Bird with porthole windows and chrome rims and etc. down, down the wide V in the middle of the bridge, carefully, slowly, s-l-o-o-o-w-l-y, and it seems to him the bridge has sagged even more since the last time (son of bitch, easy, s-l-o-w-l-y, s-l-o-o-o-w-l-y, come on . . .). The bridge is sagging so much the glare of his headlights barely extends to the opposite end.

"MOSCAS! NO MORE THUNDERBIRD!"

José looks up, sees a man at the far end of the bridge walking towards him, arms outstretched, and because of the limited range of the Thunderbird's headlights, the man has no head ("¡A la chingada! ¡El Hombre sin Cabeza!"), his hands dripping blood, and swearing he'll destroy the Thunderbird ("Bullshit!"). José lurches into action: ("¡Reverse, chinga'o! ¡First, chinga'o! ¡Reverse, chinga'o!").

"(Buzz) MOSCAS! NO MORE THUNDERBIRD!"

"¡Reverse, chinga'o!"

Something was wrong. Mosco began to think God had forsaken him. This was not heaven; it was hell, and he was being locked out again as a punishment for his sins.

But then he recognizes that smell. Tires burning!

Ah, yes. It's perfectly clear! He has to walk over the burning sinners in hell in order to inherit the Kingdom of Heaven!

The cherry-red T-Bird with porthole windows, chrome rims, etc. finally lurched out of the V. First the left rear lights and fender were smashed, then the entire left side was scraped and crunched against the steel railings, then it ricocheted clear across to the other side of the bridge where first the right rear lights and fender were battered then the entire right side was crunched and smashed into the railing, and finally it came to a stop.

"(Buzz) NO MORE THUNDERBIRD FOREVER!"

"¡Reverse, chinga'o!"

The spider gears clanged, whinnied, brayed, shuddered, and then clanged again, metal crunching, crushed by metal.

And then José noticed that attached to the body was a cabeza. That not too far behind were two more cabezas coming into his headlights, the only things on his cherry-red T-Bird with porthole windows, chrome rims, and etc. that seemed to work. "No, no, no, no, NO!"

At one A.M., Father Schmidt arrived at the old church with Monsignor Chávez, who had driven the sixty miles from Albuquerque in even less time than when he had rocketed down to San Miguel to see the burning rosary, driving Caruso into a bout of depression that he finally overcame at the next demolition derby. He had been unable to cross at the bridge because it was sagging so much it seemed ready to collapse, and he had to circle back by way of Los Brasos, where he almost crashed head-on with Caruso, who had been at the church along with the same faithful who had congregated outside Mosco's house during his last milagro. When Mosco and his sons arrived, Caruso had driven them back to the bridge, hooked the Thunderbird, and soared through the llano, where El Hombre sin Cabeza roamed on a moonless night such as this, back to San Miguel in a time that would have made Monsignor Chávez shudder with envy. The faithful were kneeling on the scarred earth, holding candles, praying rosary after rosary.

The skeptics, of course, were gathered in the rear, arguing about Mosco, placing bets.

La Tortilla Chamuscada
de La La La Chevalier

Sheriff Sapo Sánchez was writing ticket after ticket outside her house for illegal parking and driving the wrong way on a one-way street. And María Martínez was calling and offering as much as five hundred dollars (less than the amount she had paid Mosco Zamora for that "rattlesnake" hide, and that certainly was no milagro!). Caruso was offering a year's worth of free towing. Mosco was offering, for a hundred dollars, advice on how to handle the press, as well as the stress, of being at the very center of a milagro as well as suggesting she get married. *Time* magazine was pestering her for an interview. *Look* was offering her top dollar for a picture of her holding the tortilla. The monsignor was driving down from Albuquerque. Father Schmidt was leading the faithful in prayer on her front lawn. To think that only yesterday she had wanted to end her life. ¡Ay, pero Dios era tan grande! Today, oh glorious day, she was alive, and just as importantly, it was Lukie (née Jean Luc Chevalier à Paris, 1929), her dearly departed Lukie, faithful husband of twenty-five years, who was responsible. ∎

Lukie had been dead only a year, but that year had been the loneliest of her life.

La La La had decided the previous morning (though she wasn't aware of it then) that she would end her life before Mauricio got home from work. It didn't seem to matter that she had nine wonderful children (Mauricio, the youngest, was still living at home). Sí, nine wonderful children who had given her eighteen grandchildren. No matter that ending her life went against the teachings of the Catholic Church. What would Father Schmidt think? Oh, no matter.

It was only when she began to prepare Mauricio's breakfast before he went to work that she realized how she would end it all: she would leave the gas on. That should be pretty painless. And pretty fast.

All she wanted was to join Lukie. She had never been so lonely (they had met in Tennessee, of all places, and had married a year to the day later, honeymooned in Paris, and never grown apart). ▪

At about three o'clock she cleaned and put the frijoles to cook. She defrosted some green chile, peeled it, and prepared it with garlic. She prepared some red chile with small chunks of beef, exactly the way Mauricio liked it (what could she have been thinking? as if Mauricio would sit down to eat after he found her).

Then she made the masa and began flattening out some tortillas. She had made three or so, all a little burned (no matter). She turned the next one over and saw what truly could only be interpreted as a sign from God that she should live.

On it was scorched the likeness of her dear Lukie! ▪

She had fallen to her knees and wept. There was no mistaking it. This was a sign. A milagro!

She had called Father Schmidt immediately. He had driven over and heard her confession, given her communion.

Father Schmidt had inspected the tortilla thoroughly. It was impossible, he was sure, to trace such a likeness with so much accuracy and precision. And certainly La La La was not a woman of guile. No, clearly the devil would have a difficult time finding work in this woman's house.

He called the monsignor in Albuquerque, who, although skeptical, sped to San Miguel. He also called Mauricio at work, and Mauricio got permission to leave from the foreman, Chango Vásquez. Chango told Lolo and Lolo told Chato. Chato called his fiancé, La Cuca Rocha, who called Caruso. Caruso told Sapo as

Sapo wrote out a ticket for "espeeding." And Sapo called María Martínez, and etc., etc., etc. ▪

To this day the tortilla is in her living room, next to a photo of her dear Lukie—so unbelievably striking in resemblance—preserved forever in Saran Wrap.

The Election

It was one of those offices nobody really thought about much at election time. It wasn't of great importance like that of governor, whose duty it was to raise taxes and promise good roads. Or even that of lieutenant governor, who was elected to promise good roads while the governor went fishing. And certainly it wasn't as important as that of state senator, who promised to get the governor to lower taxes and put in paved roads to all the villages around San Miguel. Or as important as that of the políticos who were sent to Congress promising to talk to the president about lowering taxes and building new roads. Now those were important positions. But just a minute. Did not Justo Peña, who had been justice of the peace for as long as anybody could remember, levy fines on all cars bearing plates from Texas and New York (whether they were speeding or not)? So maybe it was a pretty important position after all, ¿qué no? In any case Justo was getting so old he was beginning to let the turistas get by with only a small fine and a long lecture. A miscarriage of justice to be sure. So when Justo announced he was retiring from office, the only subject of conversation, the only question asked was: Who would be his successor?

In a town like San Miguel where everybody knew everybody else's business, that kind of suspense was unbearable, like suffering an itch on some unreachable part of your back for two months. Finally, a week before the election, two candidates were announced: La Wedding Bells (running as a Republicana) and Billy Cates (Demócrata). Little did the citizens of San Miguel realize that that race would be if not the most uneventful, then certainly the closest in the entire political history of the town. In the end only two votes would separate the victor from the also-ran. ▪

Would it be La Wedding Bells who:

— when addressing the voters, asked them, "Who likes hay more—horses or fire?";

— took coins out of the collection box at Sunday Mass;

— swore she died once and went to Heaven for three days;

— painted lines down the backs of her legs with an eyebrow pencil to make it look like she was sporting brand-new nylons;

— said, quoting Hoover, that "The depression was only a temporary halt in the posterior of a great people." (Hoover actually said "prosperity.");

— wondered what it was like to bathe in fire;

— quoted FDR: "Democracy is not static electricity. It is an everlasting match." (What FDR really said was: "Democracy is not a static thing. It is an everlasting march.");

— asked: "If only the Demócratas were taxed, would God Bless America?";

— when pressed, said her campaign slogan was, "Tax only the Demócratas and a chicken in every pot";

— asked the voters to consider: "If Jesus Christ had been a Republicano, would the roads leading to Heaven be in the same condition as the roads leading to and from San Miguel?";

— had twelve children with her first husband, Jesús, all named after the Apostles;

— claimed her chickens were lazier than her second husband;

— promised her voters (quoting Hoover again, who said, "From a full dinner pail to a full garage"): "A garage full of palas";

— who, all of a sudden, sat up in her coffin during her velorio and said "I do";

— was afraid to use vanishing cream;

— wore her wedding gown to each of her husbands' funerals; and who . . .

— had eyes that were a perilous blue when she wore blue;

— had a second husband who was struck blind by a bolt of lightning and exactly a year later was struck again and regained his sight;

— had eyes that were enticing, judicious Paris green when she wore green;
— had a third husband who tied the church-bell rope around his neck and flung himself off the tower during an eclipse;
— was really named Ysabel Campa;
— had a fourth husband who drank holy water, thinking it would purge him of his sins;
— had a fifth husband who was a little man with nervous, hopeless eyes and equally nervous hands that fluttered away from him constantly like distracted butterflies;
— had a sixth husband who fell from a ladder while painting and thereafter insisted he was dissolving day by day;
— had fierce reddish-brown hair (that seemed to be reaching for her nalgas), which she set on fire to show her seventh husband the world as we can imagine it rather than as we know it. ▪

Or would it be Bill Cates who:
— had an immense dissatisfaction with cause and effect;
— said a man is either a drunk or a hero;
— painted portraits of nude women from Albuquerque in his studio filled with squawking parrots as he sought to "make invisible the visible";
— also said that for the Republicanos government is a contradiction between a historical and a social mission, filled with the rhetoric of subversion of the public will through the posing of ambiguous rhetorical questions;
— said additionally that the economic philosophy of the Republicanos can be classified as the theory of the absent whole;
— was free of any theological pretensions;
— furthermore, said that the philosophy of the Republicanos towards the poor was that of a thought without a thought, an aim without a target;
— also said that the Republicanos see national consciousness as profound anarchism contradicted by wholesale consumerism;
— stated that language is useless because it does not really exist; information is degraded as it is passed along, exponentially,

paradoxically, polemically, and transverbally, becoming extraneous and at the same time poetic, loaded with malicious or discursive stimuli;

— insisted that time was reversible; the difficulty lay in distinguishing the normal from the perverse. ▪

THE DEBATE

"In this election," Bill said, getting the debate underway, "you'll hear two visions: theirs is to look inward. Ours is to look forward, to restore the social fabric . . ."

"To look forward," La Wedding Bells said—not realizing that Bill and the audience could hear her—and jotted this in her notebook.

"We begin with a simple fact: government is too big and spends too much," Bill went on.

"Too big and spends too much."

"What we need," Bill pointed out, "is to control costs by cutting paperwork."

". . . by cutting paperwork," La Wedding Bells said, assuredly.

"We need relief from taxation, regulation, and litigation," Bill said, beginning to warm up.

". . . li-ti-ga-tion," La Wedding Bells said as she jotted it down, slowly, very carefully.

"We don't need my opponent's plan for a massive government takeover," Bill cautioned.

"Don't need it." La Wedding Bells said, shaking her head vigorously.

"I'll ask the state legislature to put a lid on mandatory spending . . ."

"A lid . . ."

"We are rebuilding our roads and providing more jobs . . ."

"Rebuilding roads and jobs . . ."

"And we are taking a stand for family values . . ."

"Stand for family values."

"The world is in transition, and we are feeling that transition in our homes."

"Transmissions in our homes," said La Wedding Bells, pausing, wishing she had come up with something as clever as that.

"So we have a clear choice," Bill went on. "Do we turn to the bureaucracy of the Republicanos . . ."

". . . or give people the freedom and incentive to build security for themselves?"

". . . freedom and incentive . . ."

"And so we offer a philosophy that puts faith in the individual . . ."

". . . faith and philosophy . . ."

". . . and not in the bureaucracy."

"Y no en los burros."

"A philosophy that empowers people to do their best . . ."
"Their best."

". . . so that America can be at its best."
"The best."

"In a world that is safer and freer . . ."

"Free beer." Again, that expression on her face that said, "Now why didn't I think of that?"

". . . this is how we will build an America that is stronger, safer, and more secure. Muchas gracias."

"¡Stronger and seguro que sí!"

And then the moderator from the League of Women Voters announced that La Wedding Bells was to state her political philosophy.

"In this election," she began, "you'll hear two versions: theirs is to look ingrown. Ours is to look foreign, to retry the social fabric.

"We begin with a simple fact: government is too goddam big and spends too goddam much." (PAUSE—APPLAUSE)

"What we need is to control costs (PAUSE—APPLAUSE) by cutting paperwork!

"We need relief from taxation, irregularities, and laxativitation. (PAUSE—APPLAUSE)

"And etcetera, etcetera, etcetera." ■

THE RALLY

Now it so happened that the governor was scheduled to make a very brief stop in San Miguel on his dreaded but politically necessary last-minute whirlwind tour of that godforsaken county that had the worst roads this side of hell. He would endorse the candidates, make the same promises everybody had heard since quién sabe cuando, and there would be plenty of beer and barbecue afterwards to keep everybody in good spirits.

But when María Martínez, the mayor's wife and chairwoman of the San Miguel County Republican Party, got a call that the governor was delayed, she decided to kick off the evening by having the candidates running for the smaller offices deliver their speeches first, getting the underlings out of the way immediately and allowing time for the governor's speech as the highlight of the evening.

The first to speak was Sapo Sánchez, the incumbent candidate for sheriff, who gave a long-winded speech about how safe the town had been since he had been elected and how safe the town would continue to be if he were to be reelected. Not to mention how much revenue he had brought in through "contributions" from traffic citations. At that point Caruso Zamora, his opponent, who won the demolition derby Saturday night after Saturday night and who had been issued more traffic citations than anybody in all of San Miguel County, quickly pointed out all the mistakes Sapo had made. "Errors in judgment, perhaps," Sapo said. "Pendejadas," Caruso countered, and Sapo called him a liar and threatened to arrest him right then and there. "What the hell was Caruso doing at a Republican rally anyway?" he asked himself. Caruso was trying to intimidate an officer of the law, and that was a violation of Civil Code Two Nineteen Point One; as well as creating a public disturbance, a Two Twenty-One Point Two; as well as a Two Twenty-Two Point Three, vagrancy; not to mention a Two Nineteen Point Nine, contributing to the delinquency of a minor/minors, and, no—it wasn't the beer talking, and it wasn't the badge neither. It was the best goddam sheriff this town had ever had, that's who—a Republicana who could whip any Demócrata's ass any day of the week and he was willing to prove it, "right here and now, goddammit."

And so they went at it, Sapo putting all his three hundred pounds behind one punch, meaning to end it all right then and there, but Caruso ducked and Sapo knocked over the large pot of barbecue beans, and as he pivoted and let fly a wild left hook, he slipped and knocked over the large pot of potato salad.

Sapo got up and threw another hook, slipped, and crashed into the podium, demolishing it, got up again, this time crashing into the mariachis, who were about to launch into "Happy Days Are Here Again" (at the request of María Martínez), flattening a guitar, a violin, and the lead vocalist. Then Sapo made one last great effort to knock his Democratic opponent out of the race. He got up slowly, deliberately, but slipped again, and on the way down his hand slapped his genuine leather holster and his gun went off, and La Wedding Bells, who had been standing next to the beer keg all night, went down with a terrifying scream. The crowd began running towards the door, desperate to get out, but everybody kept slipping on the beans, the potato salad, and on the quickly running rivulet of beer snaking its way down the middle of the hall. María Martínez was trying desperately to restore order. She ordered the mariachis to play. They launched into "Happy Days Are Here Again," sounding like a cross between the howl of a castrated coyote and a shriek even more bloodcurdling than that of La Wedding Bells.

Somebody shouted, "Call for an ambulance! La Wedding Bells has been shot!" "Murderer!" Caruso cried out to Sapo. "¡Cobarde!"

Several people managed to slip and slide and swim towards La Wedding Bells. "She's alive!" somebody shouted. The bullet had hit the keg, missing her by only an inch or so. "She's alive!" a woman shouted, and La Wedding Bells came to. She was helped up and, seeing that people were applauding, took this as her cue. "Ladies and gentlemen," she began, "and gentlemen and ladies. I'm Belle, and I'm running for justice of the peace. Would you rather vote for me, or for that little cabrón over there?" She pointed towards the door, where the governor happened to be standing, flanked by two huge, menacing bodyguards, poised, ready to draw their guns if one more of these hicks made any move that could be interpreted as threatening. The blond one, who had the missing teeth, broken nose, and steely eyes of an ex–middle linebacker, had completely eclipsed Bill Cates. (Now what the hell was Cates doing here at a Republican rally? La Wedding Bells wondered.)

María Martínez motioned for the mariachis to stop. "Ladieees and gentlemeeen," she announced. "Let's give the governor a warm San Miguel welcome!" Those who could got to their feet and clapped. The governor waved, smiled. La Wedding Bells continued: "In this election you'll hear two visions . . ."

"On behalf of the people of San Miguel, Governor, I'd like to welcome you," María Martínez shouted as she motioned to the mariachis to stop their braying.

". . . theirs is to look inward," continued La Wedding Bells. "Ours is to look forward!"

"Let's let the governor know who we want sitting up there in Santa Fe, sitting straight and square in the governor's chair," screamed María Martínez.

". . . to restore our social fabric," La Wedding Bells went on, undaunted.

"Let's invite the governor up with a warm welcome," María Martínez persisted, waving to the mariachis to stop. Oh, what she had to endure for the sake of the party!

"We begin with a simple fact . . . ," affirmed La Wedding Bells, "and I say to you, the challenge is to make this a better world, and so forth, for ourselves, as it were, and for those who will live in the world after us, if there is a world after us, that is to say, world without end. Amen. Sign on the dotted line with liberty and justice for all. God shed his grace on thee and etcetera, etcetera, etcetera."

María Martínez was so relieved La Wedding Bells (that bitch) had finished, and thank God those idiotas had finally stopped playing, but before she could utter another word, La Wedding Bells was singing the National Anthem, and the crowd was trying either to get to or to stay on its feet. The entire contents of the keg had been emptied by then, and the beer was lapping at the doorway, where the governor stood, searching for a gracious way to get the hell out of this godforsaken one-horse town.

When the whistling and clapping subsided, he began: "Because of my tight schedule, I find myself forced to address you from here and then dash to my waiting car."

Those who had managed to get to chairs now had to turn them around. Faithful party members slid under chairs and each other.

The governor looked anxiously at his watch.

He began: "We begin with a simple fact: government is too big and spends too much. What we need is to control costs by cutting paperwork. And etcetera, etcetera, etcetera." ▪

THE RESULTS

María, not only the wife of the Honorable Mayor of San Miguel but the precinct chairwoman as well, was the first to learn the results. The news spread through town faster than fire devouring a pile of dry tumbleweeds. Bill had been declared the winner, and despite all the speculation, the race wasn't even close. He had captured every single vote: his own, of course, and that of La Wedding Bells.

El Doctor de la Mente, a Drop of ETOH, and Etc., Etc.

The news spread faster than yesterday's gossip. The new doctor was coming!

Everybody down at La Golondrina slowly sipping their chilled wine and tap beer heard it from Mosco, who had missed work (absolutamente not another day absent from work the rest of the year, he assured his wife Matilda and his foreman at the mine). Mosco had been at the San Miguel County Health Clinic when Adelaida Martínez, the registered nurse and clinic administrator, got the call.

"Yes, Doctor Martínez, how are you? Fine, thank you. Oh, that's too bad. Yes, we do. No, no, I can call him from here much easier. It won't take him long at all, believe me!"

Then: "Hello, Tina. Could you get me Caruso's Garage, please? Thank you. Hello, Caruso, this is Adelaida. Mira, the new doctor just called. His Jeep broke down. Just this side of Las Golondrinas. Sí, towing him would be much faster. Gracias." And then Caruso at his garage, before jumping into his tow truck (he would go almost to Las Golondrinas and return to San Miguel, towing the Jeep on the way back in less than half an hour!) told Miguel Anaya, who was getting his wipers fixed in order to pass his driver's test. And, of course, then Caruso also told Sheriff Sapo Sánchez while Sapo was writing him a ticket for "espeeding." Sapo called the mayor on his radio, and His Honor promptly called his wife, María Martínez, down at The Emporium. Meanwhile, Miguel Anaya had stopped off at Jennifer Craig's Café and Grill, Mexican and American Foods, for a cup of coffee to steel him for the driving exam with Sapo and had spread the word there to the highway crew on their early morning coffee break and to the ranchers in town to conduct business, the waitresses, the cooks, Wolfgang and his wife, la Julia Yglesias, the busboys, the bus drivers, and the busybodies.

María Martínez immediately called Chucho, her chief editor at the *San Miguel Tribune,* and told him to be ready to take photos of herself and the mayor with the new doctor for the front page, welcoming him on behalf of the county, the town, the Ladies' Auxiliary, the San Miguel County Republicans, the Jaycees, the PTA, the DAV, the American Legion, and the Lions and Rotary Clubs, and Chucho immediately called Chucha with his news flash down at the bakery, and Chucha mentioned it to Mosco Zamora, but he had already heard about the new doctor twice, once at the clinic and the other from Ted Turner. Mosco had been at Ted Turner's Radio Sales and Repair Shop looking for a used TV. The tubes on his set were bien fried. Ted had been at the bakery having a cup of coffee (black, six sugars) and two donuts (chocolate covered and glazed) when Adelaida had called Lulu. Mosco had mentioned to Ted that he looked forward to meeting the new doctor because he wasn't just a doctor. He was un doctor de la mente, and Mosco knew about doctores de la mente. After all, he had been examined by one during the war (in Paris, in the springtime).

In the meantime, María Martínez had called La Lulu, La Lili, y La La La, La Lupe, and of course, La Lola, who had called Yoya, who, in turn, had phoned Tacha and Ticha and Tina, who had called Nina, who told everybody at the bank, including Pancho y La Pancha, the cashiers. And Panfilo and Perfecto, who had been in line cashing their disability checks, told Beto and Neto down at the barbershop, who had already heard about the new MD from Miguel Anaya, who had cruised by in a brand new Cadillac that he was taking for a "test drive" (see if Sapo could find anything wrong with this car!) from Madman Martínez's (the mayor's brother-in-law, No Payments for Two Years!) Car Lot, and Lalo heard it from Lolo; Louie learned about it from Lino; Beto from his cousin Beta at the furniture warehouse; and Waldo from Willie, and etc.

Caruso came to a neck-wrenching halt in the clinic parking lot and escorted the new doctor inside. "Dr. Sánchez! Welcome! ¡Bienvenido!" Adelaida exclaimed. She immediately informed him that an emergency call had just come in from Las Animas, a short five miles from El Dompe Viejo (or Farnsworth Arroyo, according to the official state map). It was Ysabel Campa, otherwise known as La Wedding Bells (sigh), a clinic "regular" who was reportedly on her deathbed. Adelaida expressed her regrets about "presenting" him with a case when he wasn't "officially" on duty, but (again, sigh, a pause so that the MD would say, "Oh, that's quite alright," which is exactly what the good doctor said). Then Dr. Sánchez asked to see the patient's file so he might review it on the way (Caruso was going to be kind enough, sigh, to drive him). ▪

As soon as Caruso bolted out of the parking lot, Adelaida was on the phone to Elisa Chacón at the unemployment office. "Yes, very handsome," and Elisa called Eleanor at the probation office. "Yes, tall, about six feet or so, and black, wavy hair." And Eleanor, of course, called Elena at the drugstore: "A big nose, but straight, high cheekbones, eyebrows como el Cary Grant," and Elena dialed Flora at the Beauty Shop. "Oh yes, very soft-spoken, y muy bien educado," and Flora spoke to Senaida at the bank: "Harvard School of Medicine," and Senaida to Yolanda, at the Dairy Queen: ". . . paying off his government loan," and Yolanda reported to Luisa, "a psychiatrist and a doctor," and Luisa to Carla: "Yes, one of us, finally" (he spoke Spanish), and Carla to Josefina, "originally from Albuquerque," and Tina, who had listened in on every single call, said, "Pobrecito, he hadn't been in town ten minutes and they had already sicced La Wedding Bells on him," and Father Schmidt called Sapo, who had just finished administering a driving exam to Miguel Anaya (who did not pass—at least five infractions before they had driven a block), and Sapo called, and etc., etc. ▪

Ysabel Campa had been named Belle—oh, she was beautiful!— in the third grade by Mrs. Scholes, who hailed from Mississippi, and the name clung to her forever after. The wedding part she got because of her six (to date) marriages. For some reason or other (most likely nerves, exhaustion), husband after husband had died on her. Her first marriage was to Jesús Chávez. They had twelve children (all named after the Apostles). Jesús died at thirty-three, when La Wedding Bells was twenty-seven or so. Then she married Fernando Benavidez, and that lasted three years. They had Alberto, Alejandro, Abrán, and Alejandrina and Alfonso (twins). After that she married Tomás Martínez, and that marriage sputtered along like an old Ford with worn-out spark plugs for three years. They had Benjamín, Bártolo, y Bártola. Then it was Placo Gutiérrez, followed by Mario Gomez, and now she was married to Botas Meadas, for about a year or so, but he had been threatening to leave. Every time he packed she went to the clinic, and the clinic then had to ship her to Albuquerque, where she was kept under observation for a week or two and then released.

Oh, if you had seen her in her youth! She was beautiful! Long brown hair. Eyes that changed color! If she wore green, her eyes would be green. Ojos de gato. And so tall and thin, a nose como la Rita Hayworth. Lips the color of ripe chokecherries. And pregnant all the goddam time since her first marriage, it seems.

Sometime in her first marriage, she began to draw lines down the backs of her legs to make it look like she was wearing nylons. She plucked out her eyebrows, cut her hair, and began smoking, and talking como la Bette Davis. ▪

As Dr. Sánchez reviewed the chart (it was extremely difficult to read the handwriting of the previous physicians who had treated La Wedding Bells, and the rocking of the tow truck as Caruso skimmed across the llano made it next to impossible), he realized the prognosis was poor at best. Worse than that: This was his first patient in San Miguel County. The outcome of the case was going to determine how the rest of the his four years here would go. It would mean people from every corner of the county coming (and more importantly, returning) for treatment, or people being frightened away, not because of his failure as a doctor, a healer with scientific methodology and knowledge, but as a psychiatrist. ▪

Caruso sped up the embankment then bounced onto the dirt road that wound its way up and down dry gullies to Las Animas. He came to a whiplash halt in front of La Wedding Bells's house, a rooster tail of dust trailing behind him.

Dr. Sánchez was led solemnly into the crowded sala by Botas Meadas, who immediately informed him that his wife had died only a few minutes before. Father Schmidt was sadly administering the last rites. Dr. Sánchez offered his condolences. Botas Meadas introduced him to the family and friends that had gathered to pray for La Wedding Bells, then offered Dr. Sánchez something to drink and urged him in the direction of the kitchen, where the tables were full of bowls of frijoles, salads of all types, tamales, burritos, platters of pies, cakes that the vecinos and friends of the family had brought as prescribed by custom. Dr. Sánchez declined politely and asked instead to be shown to the patient's room.

Dr. Sánchez walked in just as Father Schmidt was finishing the last rites. He introduced himself, and Father Schmidt shook his hand, welcomed him, and expressed his sympathy that their first meeting had to be like this, but the Lord worked in mysterious ways.

Her medical records had revealed to Dr. Sánchez a woman with a long history of constantly seeking out doctors. It was quite apparent that she had led a life as complicated and chaotic as her medical history. Problems with interpersonal relationships, noted one doctor. A long history of marital difficulties.

Cardiopulmonary symptoms: palpitations, chest pain, dizziness. Pain: joints, extremities.

Pseudoneurological symptoms: deafness, double vision, memory loss, seizures/convulsions, loss of voice, blurred vision, and paralysis or muscle weakness.

Gastrointestinal symptoms: nausea, vomiting spells, bloating.

Female reproductive symptoms: menstrual irregularities, hospitalizations.

Dr. Sánchez said "uh-huh" to himself. He would ask the family members for more information to confirm his diagnosis. He scooped the stethoscope out of his bag, checked for a pulse, and said "uh-huh" softly again. He asked the oldest daughter for a history of the mother's illnesses, and the daughter did so even though she wondered why any of that mattered now. The daughter's long history of her mother's illnesses and troubles confirmed his diagnosis.

Dr. Sánchez asked the oldest daughter to leave the room, then he removed the coins from Ysabel's eyes. "Uh-huh," he said again to himself. She had all the symptoms: overly dramatic behavior, overreaction to minor events, incessantly drawing attention to herself, and an exaggerated expression of emotions. In addition it appeared she was egocentric, self-indulgent, and oftentimes inconsiderate of others. She was also quite dependent, extremely demanding, vain, helpless, and constantly seeking reassurance, and she seemed to be prone to manipulative suicidal gestures. Diagnosis: clearly psychosomatic disorder with an underlying histrionic personality. Convincing the county about the effectiveness of psychiatry was going to be easy. What was going to be troublesome was getting this woman to come in for treatment.

He dipped into the bag, grabbed a bottle of alcohol, poured some into the cap, drew a little into the dropper, and then carefully tilted Ysabel's head upward and squeezed a drop into her nostril.

Ysabel's eyes popped open, and she sat up as if she had been rear-ended by Caruso's tow truck.

Dr. Sánchez introduced himself in Spanish and asked her how she was feeling.

"Okay," Ysabel said, looking around, not quite sure where she was and noticeably wary of the young man.

Dr. Sánchez waited until she was a little more comfortable then introduced himself again. He informed her he was the new doctor and that she was his first patient.

"A rookie, eh?"

"Yeah," the young doctor said. "A rookie."

After an uncomfortable pause, Dr. Sánchez told Ysabel he had gone over her chart on his wild ride to her house.

"Quite a chart!" he exclaimed in mock amazement.

"Quite a life!" she replied.

"Sí," Dr. Sánchez agreed, "quite a life." He paused again, overwhelmed. "A lot of ups and downs, I suppose?"

"Ooooooh," she exclaimed, "more ups and downs than a puta's panties on payday!"

Dr. Sánchez laughed heartily. "Now that's a lot of ups and downs!"

"You'd better believe it!"

Dr. Sánchez posed a question: "More ups than downs?"

Ysabel thought awhile. Then, sadly, "More downs. A hell of a lot more downs."

"You've said 'I do' a lot, haven't you?"

"I do. I do. I do. I do. I do. And I do." She paused and then said, "I guess I forgot that old refrán."

"Which one?"

"Vale más bien quedada, que mal casada."

"Y vale más arrear, que no la carga llevar."

"Vamos a ver, dijó el ciego," she countered.

"Viejo que se cura, cien años dura."

"Ir por lana, y volver trasquilado," she warned.

"Hombre prevenido, nunca fue vencido."

"La mujer y el vidrio, siempre corren peligro."

"Haciéndose el milagro, aunque lo haga el diablo."

"Zorra vieja no cae en trampa."

"Yo no suelto la cola, aunque me cagen la mano."

"Bueno," Ysabel said. She was beginning to like this young man. She would give him a chance. "Ya que la casa se quema, vamos a calentarnos."

"Entonces, I'll see you in my office in, oh, give me a couple of days to get set up. We'll review your medication. And talk. ¿Bueno?"

"Bueno. Gracias."

"I'm the one who should be saying gracias. You don't know what you've done for my career. Con permiso. I'm going to step out now. You come out when you're ready."

"Just give me a minute. I need to fix myself up a little. Compuesta, no hay mujer fea." ▪

Ysabel combed her hair quickly, a dab of lipstick, rouge, but did not give the backs of her legs more than a quick glance and then walked out into the sala.

"¡Milagro!" a vecina shrieked, and fell to her knees. "Padre nuestro," she began, and family and friends slumped to their knees just as the neighbor had. Father Schmidt led them in song: "Yo creo Dios Mío, que estás en el altar . . . ¡Bendito sea Dios! ¡Bendito sea Dios!"

Caruso sped up the embankment then bounced onto the dirt road that led to the highway. He hadn't been on the highway more than ten seconds when he heard the frantic shrieking of Sapo's siren, the lights flashing hysterically, just like the midway during the county fair. "That's a violation of CC, that's Civil Code 351, Caruso, espeeding, and a violation of CC, that's Civil Code 472, eswerving," Sapo intoned, chins quivering.

While he wrote out the citation (and Dr. Sánchez wrote in his notes the medical shorthand for a drop of alcohol: i gtt ETOH), Caruso explained to Sapo how Dr. Sánchez had just performed a milagro.

"Este hombre revive los muertos," he said, and gave Sapo an account of the afternoon's milagro. Then Sheriff Sapo called the mayor on the radio, and the mayor called María Martínez immediately, and María Martínez called Flaco, who called María Elena, who wasn't impressed. Meanwhile Caruso had told Miguel Anaya while he was working on his turn signals, and Miguel told Mosco Zamora, and Mosco Zamora told Ted Turner, etc., etc.

Tía Adelaida Goes to San Antone

I was eleven years old when Tía Adelaida's niece, Marta, and her husband, Clint, came to take her to San Antone. I couldn't fully understand what they were up to, mostly because they were using a lot of big words that I later learned belonged to the worlds of law and business. But I understood fully that they were stealing her away on the pretext that they wanted to care for her in her old age. Once they got her to San Antone, I was sure they would get her to sign her house and land over to them. I was certain she was aware of Clint and Marta's scheme. I simply could not understand why she would allow them to take her away without a word of protest. ▪

Tía Adelaida had lived in Los Brasos, at the foot of the mountains, her entire life. The house, with its ten acres of timberland, had belonged to the Sánchez family for several generations, since the end of the Navajo wars.

There were rumors throughout the county as far back as I could remember of the wheelbarrows full of gold waiting to be extracted from some rich vein somewhere on Tía's property. You see, Tía paid for everything in little nuggets she shook out of an old beaded tobacco pouch.

I remember that Papá was concerned about her safety because she was always followed when she walked into the surrounding forest. Once everybody learned it was impossible to keep up with her, they tried lying in wait, hoping she would walk by and lead them to the cave where she mined her gold.

In her later years, when she couldn't walk as fast and surefooted as before, Tía simply waited until nightfall and nobody was ever able to follow her for very long.

Whenever Papá voiced his concern about her, Mamá would always remind him that she was the descendent of Demetrio, the scout that chased down Victoriano, the legendary renegade Navajo. It was said that Demetrio was a Mexican who had been captured during a raid by a band of Navajo raiders when he was a young boy of eight and had been returned to San Miguel in a trade for horses several years later. ▪

Clint and Marta had arrived in their old Cadillac on Friday evening right at supper time. Papá had just walked in the door, dead tired from his shift in the mine. He seemed more than a little annoyed, not only because they showed up just as Mamá and Tía Adelaida were setting the table but also because they had the nerve to invite themselves to supper. "Sinvergüenzas," Papá muttered. "¡Juan!" Mamá scolded him. "They are family. They are welcome in this house." "They are sinvergüenzas," Papá said, "and nothing more." He then waddled off to take his hot bath.

When supper was served, Papá invited Clint and Marta to the table by saying, "Vengan a comer, sinvergüenzas," which ordinarily meant "Come and eat without any shame," but in this case it could easily be interpreted as "Come and eat, shameless ones." ▪

At first I was happy that Tía Adelaida had come to live with us only because I finally had somebody to help me feed the animals and chop firewood. As time went on, I began to like her more and more. She never complained about the many chores Papá had set aside, especially for me. She became a friend I would love forever when she began helping me with my homework, especially with my arithmetic. Papá was so impatient and demanding when it came to numbers, and, in truth, both of us were relieved when Tía Adelaida took charge of helping me learn how to add and subtract. Tía helped me not so much by providing answers but by encouraging me not to give up, to think and rethink a problem until the answer had no choice but to find its way to me.

Sometimes, after my homework was done, she would tell me the old stories about San Miguel County as she made sugar candy on the stove. While we shared the candy she drew different types of animal tracks, so that I would learn to trail as easily as reading a story or a poem.

And now and then she would draw maps with landmarks that you could not find on any official map, caves where I could find shelter from summer rainstorms or refuge from fierce snowstorms. She never failed to shred these scraps of paper and throw them into the fire. She always emphasized that what she had just shown me was a secret. I would understand when I was older, she would say, then she would wish me "buenas noches," kiss me on the forehead, and shuffle off to bed. ▪

For an entire week Clint and Marta spent their day down at the courthouse. They came home with accordion files full of old documents that they discussed in secretive tones late into the night. ▪

When Tía Adelaida came to live with us, I was the only one she allowed to carry the statue of San Antonio from her house. Oh, how she loved San Antonio! And oh, how she could show her disappointment with him when he failed to grant her a favor!

When she asked him for a favor—and she never asked for anything that was beyond the good saint's power—San Antonio always seemed to answer her in mysterious but wonderful ways. But when he seemed to be taking a little too long, Tía would turn him around in his nicho and let him face the wall until he saw fit to grant her the favor or until Tía realized there were solutions that she herself could provide.

Sometimes San Antonio would get stubborn, and that's when Tía Adelaida got so angry she would punish him more severely than simply having him face the wall. Once, when Mamá scooped some frijoles for supper out of the large can in the kitchen, out came San Antonio! Who knows how long he had been sentenced to the lonely darkness.

Oh, they had their quarrels! But they had the kind of quarrels where the combatants truly respected and loved one another. ▪

Marta, it seems, was a distant cousin of Tía Adelaida's. When she would mention all the old names, tears would come to Tía's eyes. Old names. Tío Santiago, Primo Flavio, Tía Josefita. ■

Summer was the greatest time of all. Papá would drop Tía Adelaida and me off at Tía's old house on his way to work early in the morning. Tía would show me the tracks I had learned at the kitchen table. I also learned how to fashion hooks out of thorns to catch fish as well as how to build traps, how to build a fire, and how to cook outdoors. As we traveled over her land, she would gather plants and roots in an old gunnysack and teach me their names, along with their uses—which were for cooking and which for medicinal purposes.

But most importantly, she told me the old stories of San Miguel. The story of old Demetrio and his clashes with Victoriano. The legend of Victoriano's gold mine. A story, I was to learn later, that she had related in specific detail only to me. ■

As I said before, Clint and Marta spent the entire week down at the courthouse. In the evenings, after supper, they would question Mamá and Papá about the boundaries of Tía Adelaida's land, about her government check, and about her will. Question after question about deeds and titles. Clint and Marta truly were sinvergüenzas. And more often than not, questions about Victoriano's gold. ■

On Thursday night of that week, Clint and Marta announced that they would be returning to San Antone the next day with Tía Adelaida. Interestingly enough, Tía Adelaida had already packed her clothes in an old suitcase. I could not believe that they were taking her away and that she was going with them so willingly. She was not putting up any kind of a fight, and that was really burning Papá up. But, surprisingly, he was minding his manners. He was ready to explode, but he wasn't saying a word. As for Tía Adelaida, it seemed she was puffing away on her brown-paper cigarrito without a care in the world. ■

After breakfast I kissed Tía goodbye and left for school, expecting never to see her again. I thought about her all day long in school. Miss Baca would call on me and I couldn't answer the simplest of questions. I wasn't the least bit hungry, so I gave my lunch to Coyote Sánchez.

The only question of any concern to me was why Tía seemed so willing to go with Clint and Marta. Perhaps she wanted to get to know Marta, who was, after all, a part of Tía's life that would have been denied her if Marta hadn't come to San Miguel. Perhaps Tía felt she was becoming too much of a burden on Mamá and Papá and wanted to give them some time alone. Maybe, in addition to all that, she wanted to travel—see different places.

When the bell finally rang, I dragged myself home. As I neared our house, I saw that the old Cadillac was still parked in the front yard. Clint was pacing back and forth, huffing and puffing, as if each minute was a dollar lost. Tía Adelaida had known I'd be upset and worried, so she had refused to leave until I got home from school. Once I saw her, I broke into a run. She gave me a long, strong abrazo, said "Adios, m'jito," and climbed into the back seat. As she was stepping in, her handbag opened, and there was San Antonio resting peacefully on a bed of old straw.

Johnny

Tacks

To my grandmother, Irene Sánchez Jirón

"¡SONAMABISQUETE!"

It was Uncle Hoople's voice, and it sounded like he was right there standing next to my bed even though he was in the kitchen. What a way to wake up, especially from my dream with ten seconds left in the third overtime of the state-championship game against the hated Miami Eagles.

I called my Uncle Conrado Uncle Hoople because he looked exactly like Major Hoople, the comic-strip character, especially in winter when he wore his red flannel winter cap with the flaps down and untied. Uncle Hoople had the same lump of a nose, the same beady eyes, the same huge stomach, the same way of hrrumphing whenever he said anything of importance (which was always), and, of course, the same large lard-ass.

The major difference between them, it seemed to me, was that the major seemed to possess and enjoy a sense of humor. He didn't really take himself very seriously. Well, perhaps he did, but it was obvious that we, the readers, were supposed to see through all his pompous hrrumphing. Uncle Hoople, on the other hand, never seemed to laugh unless he was criticizing somebody. What idiotas we had for mayor! And for gobernador. "¡SONAMABIS-QUETE!" Not one of the políticos we had elected to office had the slightest idea about running the city, the state, the country. We were being taxed to death. And los juvenile delinquents were taking over the country. "¡Sonamabisquetes!"

Years later I would learn of the many times Uncle Hoople had pulled another miner out seconds before a shaft caved in and of the harsh discrimination his generation had faced and endured.

Perhaps that was what had made him such a bitter man. He was, after all, an intelligent man in his own fashion and had once run for office, but lost. He didn't know the simple tricks of being a small-town político. Things like buying spoiling meat cheaply and putting it on the tables of the hungry voters of the east side.

The Uncle Hoople I knew, however, the uncle I least fancied as a role model (and the one I ended up mirroring), was the one who, every morning after I got out of my soaked bed, greeted me mercilessly as I walked into the kitchen with, "¿Cómo hace el gatito?" and then quickly, before Grandma could admonish him, answer with "meow, meow, meow," which sounded quite innocent except that in Spanish *mea'o* is a contraction for *meado*, which means "one who has peed on himself."

"¡SONAMABISQUETES!"

I folded the pillow over my head and began to drift back into my dream: "The teams break out of their huddles. Ten seconds to go, ladies and gentlemen, the San Miguel Rattlers trailing their arch-rivals, the Miami Eagles, 99 to 97, in the third overtime of the state-championship game here at Johnson Gym on the campus of the University of New Mexico, home of the New Mexico Lobos.

"Look for the Rattlers to go to their star guard, Johnny Barros. He'll milk some time off the clock then go for the win. The Rattlers line up, Lopez inbounds to Barros, who dribbles to the top of the key—EIGHT! SEVEN! Barros fakes right, evades a defender, dribbles left—SIX! FIVE! He dribbles back to the top of the key—FOUR! THREE! He drives in, pulls up for a jumper. "Flagpole" Domínguez comes flying out of the middle of the zone defense to block it, but Barros pulls it away. HE'S FOULED! Barros shoots, his high-arching jumper is on its way. BUZZZ!"

"Los juvenile delinquents. ¡SONAMABISQUETES!"

I clamped the pillow harder around my ears, and then eased my hand down towards the mattress, praying with all the fervor of a Catholic schoolboy who had memorized his entire catechism that the bed wouldn't be wet, even though I knew that it was. I would wait until Uncle Hoople left, and then I'd get up. Uncle

Hoople had been up all night working his shift in the mine. I had nothing but time. I'd stay in bed till noon. Till sundown if necessary. I let myself tumble down, down into the safety of my dream:

"It's GOOD! Barros's shot is GOOD! The Rattlers' fans have begun their celebration. A phenomenal shot at the buzzer. I hope you can hear me over the noise of the crowd, ladies and gentlemen. This place has gone berserk. Already several fistfights have broken out in the stands."

"¡SONAMABISQUETES! . . . my tire!"

"And now Barros is stepping up to the free-throw line. Suddenly, you can hear a pin drop. He bounces the ball once, twice, flips it up, catches it, the Miami coach is crunching down hard on his red-and-black towel. Barros's shot is on its way. GOOD! The Rattlers win it! Barros has just buried Miami's dreams of a second consecutive state championship! The Rattlers guaranteed their fans a championship a year ago at this time after their controversial loss to the Eagles. The Eagles went undefeated the entire season, and Barros just buried their dreams with no time remaining at the end of the third overtime."

". . . con una navaja. ¡SONAMABISQUETES!"

It was no use. I had to get out of bed. I was soaked. The smell was dreadful. I put on dry underwear and sat down on the rocking chair next to the bed as quietly as possible. I had to decide whether or not to face Uncle Hoople. Today was the day I got to play with Benny, my cousin, again. I had vowed to stay in my room until sundown if necessary, but the smell was dreadful. I was miserable and hungry, so I got up and headed down the hallway and into the kitchen like a condemned tire-slashing juvenile delinquent to his doom.

"¿Cómo hace el gatito?" Uncle Hoople inquired the instant he saw me. "Meow, meow."

By the time I finished my huevos and pan tosta'o, Grandma had already hauled in the large tin tub for my daily bath, poured in the water she heated on the wood-burning stove, drawn the shades, and stepped outside to puff on her brown-paper cigarrito.

As I stepped out to begin my day, basketball in hand, Grandma reminded me she wanted me to get her some tacks from the old Arab's store down the hill so she could patch the tears in the linoleum floor in the sala. I told her I'd go the minute she called. She had already washed the sheets in the clanging old washer, put them mercilessly through the old hand-cranked wringer, and hung them out to dry like huge flags of surrender. I'm sure Uncle Hoople's family had seen them by now, since their kitchen window faced our yard. I told Benny once when he asked that I had a rare disease whose name was too difficult to pronounce, and that stopped him from asking me anything about my bed-wetting again. Nevertheless, I still had to live with everybody seeing those sheets every morning.

This morning, a glorious summer morning, was a little different, however, because this marked the day that Benny would be allowed to play with me again, a week after the infamous game of H-O-R-S-E in Uncle Hoople's backyard. Benny was pleading as I stepped up to the free-throw line, "You've got to make it, Johnny!" He had already, by some miracle, made his stupid dipsy-do Wilt Chamberlain grammaw free throw to give Janice, his older sister, H-O-R, and she was slashing lines in the dirt, snorting like she'd eaten a spoonful of chile pequín. I sink my Bill Russell hook easily over Wilt, and Jenny, Benny's little sister, thunks the ball off the backboard into Benny's ecstatic hands. He lifts his stupid Dodgers cap, wipes the sweat from his freckled forehead, dribbles clumsily, then flips up another archless Wilt grammaw that bounces on the rim and then falls in. "It's H-O-R-S if you don't make it," he says delightedly to Janice. "You shut up, Fatso," she replies, and shoots, thud, right off the front of the rim, and Benny immediately begins chanting H-O-R-S! Janice thumps the ball off his head and he starts crying. When he gets over it he starts in again, and I immediately join him: "H-O-R-S! H-O-R-S!" Janice has picked up a handful of rocks and begins throwing them, and suddenly Jenny joins her. We're getting pelted and head for cover, yelling "HORS! HORS!" as we slip into the old outhouse an instant before a vicious barrage hits the door.

We're gasping, lungs on fire as if we've inhaled bucketfuls of lime, stomachs hurting from laughing so hard. Benny opens the door, yells "H-O-R-S!" and manages to close it just before the next bombardment. "WOO-HOOOO! HORS!" Benny sticks his head out again, yells "HOOOORS!" and again manages to slam the door shut just in time. "Son of a bitch!" Janice shouts. "Shithead!" Jenny adds, for good measure. Where in the hell is Uncle Hoople or Aunt Juana so they can hear their perfect little girls cussing? Benny thinks he's got the routine pretty well mastered, so he opens the door, gets as far as "H-O—" when a rock the size of a hockey puck thunks him right between the eyes. Benny slides down the wall in slow motion, knees buckling, blood streaming down his face just like the pictures in the wrestling magazines. Suddenly Aunt Juana comes crashing out of the house, demanding to know what happened to Benny, all the time eyeing me suspiciously. I don't know what to say or do, because I'm so used to Benny's family being right all the time that I know anything I say or do will be wrong. After all, they were a family, Dodgers fans, and I was a product of a failed marriage who had been sent to live with his grandparents, a devout Yankee fan. If I try to say something to prove my innocence, I'll look guilty; on the other hand, if I say nothing it will surely be taken as a sign of guilt. I try to think fast, but I'm tongue-tied, frozen. Aunt Juana wheels Benny inside, orders the girls in, and there is nothing else for me to do but tramp home, only eight and a half and already an incorrigible juvenile delinquent. ■

I practiced my free throws, swish, swish, swish, one right after the other, through the bicycle rim Grandpa had nailed for me over the door of the chicken coop, looking constantly to see if Benny had been allowed out of the house. When he finally came out, we waved to each other instantly and walked to the fence to talk. He was wearing a huge bandage. I was sure glad to see him, but I could tell by the look on his face that he had blamed everything on me. I was going to have to beg him a little in order for him to convince Aunt Juana it was okay to walk to the store with me. I guess I depended so much on him because after Grandma and Grandpa he was the only family I had. He was only two years older, but he knew just how to suggest something and then step aside and watch me carry it out far beyond the limits of his imagination. I was so hungry for attention, I would do whatever was necessary to grab center stage.

The problem was that I always ended up taking the rap or in some way paying dearly for his bright ideas. Take, for example, the time we lit up a cigar in the restroom under the grandstand of the racetrack. This was right after he had almost worked up the courage to ask the bartender for a beer but had luckily chickened out at the last second. After only a few puffs on the cigar, I was the one who came home and threw up violently all over Grandma's linoleum floor. I had to do some fast thinking and blamed it on the hotdogs at the concession stand, and after that I had to use all my powers of persuasion to get her to even think of letting me go to the horse races again. I had to promise I wouldn't eat there. A promise I never intended to keep and did not. And it was his prompting, of course, that led to the tacks incident, which caused me some real serious worrying. But I'm getting a little ahead of myself.

I had to ask him if I could go over to his house and play, because he was rarely allowed to come play with me on Grandma's side of the fence. He said Uncle Hoople and Aunt Juana were pretty angry because he had needed stitches, but he seemed pretty sure we could play.

I'd let him beat me at HORSE, and then I'd ask him to accompany me to the store. I threw the ball over, grabbed Grandpa's shovel, and pole-vaulted over the fence. In no time at all I had lost H-O-R-S-E to H-O. When I heard Grandma calling me again, I scaled the fence and ran and volunteered to get the tacks for her before she had to call me an exasperating third time. In the meantime Benny was going to be working on Aunt Juana.

"Toma, m'hito, aquí tienes dos reales," Grandma said as she clinked the nickels and dimes into my hands. I was to buy three boxes of tacks and return immediately. And with change. All the change. Benny was about to knock as I ran out the door. He was smiling. "My mom let me go," he announced excitedly, "but I have to go straight home afterwards."

"Okay," I said. All that meant was that the walk down the hill and back was going to take a little longer than if Grandma had gone for the tacks herself. I grabbed my basketball and quickly got a fast break going. We flew by Mrs. Romero's house across the street and were on our way.

Benny was huffing and puffing after half a block, so we slowed down, walked a block, and when we started down the hill he pulled out his pack of Oasis, lighted one, and inhaled deeply. "Aaaah," he said, soothed. Not a worry in the world. You would've thought the Dodgers had swept the Series from the Yankees four in a row.

I didn't want to be a big chicken, so I grabbed a smoke, flipped open Benny's Zippo, and got it going. I started to ask him if he wasn't worried somebody driving by might see us and report us to Uncle Hoople. I wanted to work on my dribbling, but instead I fell into step with Benny until we had smoked the cigs down to their filters. ▪

The old Arab lifted his dead left arm up to the counter, stuffed a cone into the gnarled fingers, scooped up some chocolate-swirl ice cream, handed it to me with a sly smile, then dragged his left leg across the oiled wooden floor to the cash register, punched out the sale, and dropped the change into my hand. With his gold-rimmed glasses, his green gambler's eyeshade, grey eyes, and ruffled white hair like a mad scientist's, he was easily the most colorful store owner on our side of town. A likable and kindly man.

Benny was trying to act surprised that I had been bold enough to buy the cone with Grandma's change. I mean, I was going to buy one anyway, but he managed to make his suggestion to buy it look like a dare only the biggest chickenshit would back out of, and this made me want to spend Grandma's change even more. If there was one thing I couldn't resist, it was a dare. And the little hypocrite knew it, but he went on all the while, "What if Grandma finds out? What if Grandma finds out?"

We started back home, sharing the cone, gobbling it down quickly. Benny pulled out an after-dinner cig for each of us, and we smoked all the way to the start of the hill. We decided to work on our hook shots. Suddenly, as if wondering out loud, Benny said, "You think they're big enough?"

"Is what big enough?" I asked, interrupting my fade-away game-winner.

"The tacks. You know, big enough to cause a flat."

No sooner had he finished his sentence than I flipped him the ball, dug out one of the boxes, poured two or three tacks out, quickly faked left, right, then put up a hook as easily as Russell over Chamberlain. Benny's eyes widened large as hubcaps as I dug out the box and again poured out another two or three tacks.

"What if Grandma finds out?" he asked, frightened.

"How's she going to find out?" I said, so confidently I surprised myself. I fired a quick jumper from deep in the corner: "Score tied, two seconds left, the state championship at stake—swish!" Suddenly I grew tired of basketball. After all, it was summer and summer was baseball season.

"Bottom of the ninth, Yankees lead seven to nothing," I began. "The Dodgers have a man on second. Full count on Duke Snider. There's the pitch. The Duke swings, connects, a hard-hit ball to center field—it could be outta here! It's gone! No, it's snagged at the wall! Here comes the throw to second . . ." I zinged the tacks back down the road. "The runner slides. He's outta there! The Dodgers go down in defeat. The Yanks reign as champions of baseball!"

Benny whipped out another smoke, got it going from the butt of the old one. He was beginning to get very very aggravated. The Duke was God in Uncle Hoople's house.

"You play first," I told him. "Snider hits a weak bouncer, it's scooped up, there's the routine throw to first . . ." I flipped a couple of tacks straight at him. Even Bela Lugosi avoiding garlic couldn't have moved faster than my cousin chubby Benny. "The Dodgers drop the seventh and deciding game!"

Benny was turning very very red. "Grandma's going to get mad," he warned, hoping that would get me to stop. We were at the top of the hill, and I thought I saw Grandma standing at the corner and then walking away. I fished out the other two boxes and poured out tacks until there was an equal amount in all three, swore Benny to secrecy, and then worked on my bounce passes the rest of the way home.

The instant I placed the boxes in Grandma's hand I could tell she knew something was wrong. She weighed them individually in one hand, switched them back and forth from one hand to the other, frowning more and more all the while. I pretended to look puzzled, even hurt and disappointed, as if I could not begin to understand why she would have to weigh such trivial items as a couple of boxes of tacks. Didn't she trust me?

Then she said she couldn't believe how you were getting less and less for your money these days. Maybe she hadn't seen me throwing the tacks after all. Maybe she had and she was testing me. Well, she wasn't getting anything out of me. My lips were sealed tighter than a bear trap.

I handed her the change. She frowned some more, asked if that was all, and I assured her quite sincerely that it was. She couldn't believe how expensive the old Arab was getting. Not only were you getting less, you were paying more. She was going to start taking her business elsewhere. "Sí, Grandma," I said, nodding in complete agreement. I had expected her to ground me for taking so long, but I guess the shock of paying so much and getting so little made her forget all about that. She dismissed me, and I went out to the backyard and worked on my free throws the rest of the day. ■

"¡SONAMABISQUETE! . . . puntillas . . ."

It was Uncle Hoople, and he was louder and madder than ever. Had he said puntillas? I was as good as dead. I would stay in bed for days if I had to.

I had been found out. Had Benny fingered me? I didn't think so. But under interrogation he would be the first to turn into a dirty yellow rat. And what about Grandma? Had she said anything to Uncle Hoople about sending me down the hill the day before? If so, Uncle Hoople would see to it that she locked me up forever. Oh, I was dead. No telling what was going on in the kitchen. I would have to run away from home; I would probably get caught and get sent to the reform school in Miami. I was destined to become a juvenile delinquent just like Uncle Hoople had predicted.

I pulled the pillow over my head, not because I wanted to hide but because suddenly I was laughing so hard I needed to muffle it. I realized that Grandma would always protect me and that I would never, ever in my life have to stoop to plan anybody's downfall. As much as life had hurt me, somehow I would always be protected from such things. I had been hurt in my short life, but I had never realized how much I'd also been loved.

No matter what act of vengeance I would've dared dream up, nothing—absolutely nothing—could have ever proved more satisfying than lying there that morning listening to Uncle Hoople complain about first replacing one flat with his spare, then walking to the filling station and back with one flat after another, and how he had spent the entire morning after a tiring shift in the mine (huffing and puffing), up and down the road, up and down, bent over with a large magnet.

"¡SONAMABISQUETE!"

Freedom of Speech
and the Halloween Party

One more curl and Freddy would win and settle once and for all who was gonna go to the Halloween party the next day as The Mummy. Arturo had struggled through four one-arm curls with twenty-five pounds on the barbell and now Freddy—who had huffed and puffed, not bothering to remove the Pall Mall from his mouth, huffed and puffed some more, knocking out four quick and easy reps—was pausing for effect as well as to catch his breath. He sucked in a mouthful of air and smoke and launched into the last curl, and immediately Arturo began protesting. "No fair, Freddy puto, you can't swing it behind your big fat ass, cabrón!" Freddy finished the curl and dropped the barbell casually at Arturo's feet. "¡Cabrón Freddy, truchas!" Arturo yelped as he hopped back. Freddy rolled down the sleeve of his flannel shirt and proclaimed himself the champion. "I'm The Mummy, cabrón," he muttered. "It's a tie," Arturo continued in protest. "You can't swing way back behind your big fat ass, cabrón. That's cheating!" "You're full of shit," Freddy countered. "I didn't swing it back." "You did too! Way behind your big fat ass," Arturo argued, backing away as Freddy, broad and thick and knock-kneed, a face like a bulldog with two huge fuzzy eyebrows, charged towards him, his huge fists doubled, swinging. "Ask Johnny," Arturo said, backpedaling as fast as his sparrow legs would allow him, Freddy's magnificent hooks, jabs, and "apercuts," as Arturo called them, coming in closer and closer to his knife-edged chin. Arturo was skinny and pale, a face like the jagged edge of a saw, with large, fluttering eyes like Tweety's and hair that refused combing, as stiff as the bristles of a janitor's broom. "Tell him, Johnny," he pleaded.

Whenever he found himself losing to Freddy (which was often), Arturo turned to me for help. Sister Ann, our teacher, had taught us that one of our duties as true Catholics was to tell the truth. Freddy finished a ferocious "apercut" and turned to me, fuzzy eyebrows coming together like two myopic caterpillars colliding just as they did in class whenever Sister Ann asked even the simplest of questions. "You swung it way back, Freddy," I said. Freddy lunged at me, missing my chin but clubbing me in the throat. "!Cabrón, Freddy!" I groaned. "See!" Arturo shouted triumphantly. "You cheated, you fat-ass puto!" "Ah, scre-e-ew yo-o-u," Freddy said. Arturo responded by flipping Freddy a finger. Freddy immediately flipped one in return and charged him again, this time landing an "apercut" on Arturo's sharp chin. "¡Puto!" Arturo squawked, swinging wildly. He managed to scratch Freddy's right fist as Freddy came in with one of his punches, and Freddy called him a putito who didn't know how to fight, and Arturo told him, "Come on and get your apercuts," and Freddy held the front of his khakis and told him, "Here's some apercuts for you, putito!" Arturo said, "Those aren't apercuts, they're piñones. These are apercuts." Freddy faked another apercut but swung his enormous leg back instead and caught Arturo in the groin with the tip of his scuffed army boot. Arturo plopped to the ground. "¡Aiiiee, cabrón!" he cried as he went down, both hands cupped lovingly over his crotch. He squirmed and twisted on the ground like a Holy Roller, rubbing both hands back and forth delicately, tenderly, moaning, "mis huevos, mis huevos, Freddy Puto." He claimed he couldn't get up. He was probably "raptured."

He was going to miss the Halloween party. His eyes rolled up as far as they would go. His tongue was sticking out. Mocos were coming out of both nostrils. "Mis huevos," he continued. "Call the ambulance. I'm not bullshitting, man. I'll probably never have children. Not even a hard-on. Shit. Might as well be . . . dead." (Here a great exhalation of breath, his last.) "Oh, my God . . . heartily sorry for having offended thee. All I wanted . . . at the hour of our death . . . was to be . . . The Mummy . . ." "Hey, fuck you, Arturo!"

Freddy shouted. "I'm going as The Mummy, cabrón. And I'm gonna win the prize for the best costume."

Sister Ann had told us that we would have a thirty-second time limit. Whoever lasted the longest without being identified would win the big prize. There was also going to be a prize for the boy or girl who could identify the most masqueraders. Nobody was interested in that, because Sister Ann would probably let Cindy try to guess every single time her hand flew in her face. "Okay, Freddy, fuck you," Arturo said, jumping up swiftly, grabbing his comb out of his pocket. "You go as The Mummy. But you're gonna have to go to confession for cheating and for rapturing me, and you'll probably have to say fifty rosaries, and you know you can't count past twenty-five." "Hey, fuck you," Freddy said, tugging his leg back to kick Arturo again. "Okay," Arturo said, resigned, "then I'm going as Zorro." "Hey," I interrupted, "I thought I was—" "Hey, Johnny," Arturo said, "you only did two curls, man." There was no point in arguing. I couldn't beat Arturo up even after Freddy had raptured him. Besides, Arturo was my best friend. "Okay, you go as Zorro and I'll go as The Lone Ranger," I said. That was close enough to Zorro for me.

Then I remembered. "Hey, what about Raymundo? What's he going as?" I said. Raymundo must have been at the window, listening, because all of a sudden he strolled out, hair slicked back, high pompadour, wearing shades, his shoes spit-shined glossy, chest puffed out, pug nose high in the air as if he already drove the Jaguar he bragged he would someday own. He hadn't come out to take part in the curling contest because he knew he would win. His older brother had done about five years in the state pen for burglary, had come back beefed up, and had started Raymundo on a daily weight-lifting program.

Raymundo said he wasn't really interested in crap like costumes. That stuff was for squares. We started off for school, but Raymundo called us back. His brother (he always used his brother's rep to keep us terror stricken) wasn't going to like it if he found his weights scattered everywhere. So we stacked the weights dutifully, and then, only then, were we ready to begin our walk to St. Michael's Catholic School. ▪

Next day Raymundo came out even later than usual, so we had no choice but to get going right away. We were gonna walk into Mass late again, and Sister Frances, the principal, was going to be furious, especially when Freddy walked up the aisle, his horse-shoe taps cling-clang-ching-clanging all the way to the fifth-grade pews.

We picked up our books and shopping bags stuffed with costumes and took off down the alley, jumped over old Flaco Chávez's wire fence, and got it sagging again. We ran quickly across his yard before he could get any farther than his back porch and yell futilely, "¡Babosos, sinvergüenzas!" and threaten to kick our asses one by one. "You little shits!" he hollered. By then we had already jumped the opposite fence and were heading up the street on our way to eight o'clock Mass, with a stop for some macaroons at The Emporium, of course.

"¿Sabes qué?" Raymundo said to nobody in particular, opening up the morning's conversation. "We cuss too much." Of all of us Raymundo cussed the least, so that meant he was going to come up with something that would make him look good.

"We have to find a way to stop cussing," he continued.

"Aw, bullshit!" Freddy countered immediately. "We don't cuss that much."

"Yeah," Arturo joined in, "we don't cuss that much. That's bullshit!"

"See what I mean?" Raymundo said, triumphantly. "You guys can't say one single sentence without using a cussword."

"Bullshit!" Freddy countered again, his pride wounded.

"Hey, screw you, Raymundo," Arturo joined in.

"See what I mean?" Raymundo said, full of delight. "I rest my case. But I know how to get you guys to stop."

"How?" Freddy asked, his fuzzy eyebrows glumly collapsing together.

"Simple—we turn it into a game."

Now this was something dreamed up by somebody with brains. Raymundo was a bigger burro than Freddy. I was sure his mother had heard us cussing away every morning, had finally come up with a strategy to get us to stop, and had rehearsed it (and rehearsed it) with him.

"Oh yeah?" Freddy said. "What kind of chickenshit game?"

"Yeah, what kind of bullshit?" Arturo added.

Raymundo, ignoring them, went on: "All we have to do is give whoever cusses ten chingasos right in the shoulder."

"On the shoulder," I corrected him.

"Shit, man, let's play," Freddy bellowed.

"Yeah!" Arturo yelled, "and you get ten chingasos right away." He swung and clobbered Freddy on the shoulder.

"¡Cabrón! We weren't even playing, jodido!"

"That's twenty more!" Arturo cried out, elated.

Freddy began blocking the blows, and then it occurred to him that Arturo had been cussing too.

"Hey, you said chingasos. That's cussing!" He swung at Arturo and missed.

"Bullshit!" Arturo shouted, "chingasos ain't a cussword. Ask Johnny."

"Screw Johnny!"

"Hey," I said, "we're gonna be real late for Mass. Sister Ann is gonna kill us."

Freddy picked up his bag and swung it at Arturo. "Excuse me," he said, as the bag hit Arturo in the nuts.

"Fucker," Arturo gasped, bending at the waist, "mis huevos . . ."

"Fuck you, Zorro, from The Mummy," Freddy said, planting a kick on Arturo's ass. ▪

We rambled into church just before Father Schmidt turned around to present the host to the congregation. As Freddy cling-klanged his way up the aisle, Sister Ann's face grew redder, red hot with his every step.

Freddy stepped into the pew last, just as the row was kneeling, and as we went to our knees we swayed in unison to our left and

Pluto popped out at the other end and landed in the aisle. Sister Ann stomped up the aisle furiously and yanked Sapo off his knees. Sapo was protesting, "I didn't do nothing, Sister—honest, Sister. It was stupid Freddy," as Sister Ann led him by the ear all the way to the very last pew, where she sat him down right next to her, her sizzling glare frying him into total submission until at last, at long last, Father Schmidt muttered in his thick accent, "Go in pisz. The Mess is ended."

For whatever reason, perhaps because, like an old married couple who weren't happy unless they were quarreling, Freddy and Arturo started up again about how many chingasos one owed the other. Freddy claimed Arturo had thirty coming to him, and Arturo was certain that if he had thirty coming to him then Freddy had no less than a hundred credited to his account. "A hundred? Here's a down payment, cabrón," Freddy said, charging at Arturo. Arturo fought back with, "Here's for my layaway plan," swinging furiously, and they tangled and hit the ground, wrestling, until Sister Ann, with Cindy by her side, marched up and grabbed each by the ear and separated them, asked what the problem was, and Freddy told her, "Nothing, Sister, Arturo is my best friend and a joto jodido," and Sister turned to Cindy to translate, but before she could say anything, Freddy told Sister that meant "faithful companion, like Tonto in The Lone Ranger," and of course, not to be outdone, Arturo said Freddy was his "best friend and a real puto pendejo" and instantly translated that into "blood brother, kind of like Chingachgook on TV." Sister Ann didn't look too convinced, but I suspect she didn't really want to hear any genuine translations that early in the day, so she sent us off to the cafeteria for toast and hot cocoa before class. Freddy said, and Arturo agreed, that this was an issue to be settled after school. ■

The first contestant who walked up was obviously Willie. Everybody recognized him immediately. He was dressed as a hobo—coveralls, old hat, fuzz glued all over his face, a new tie he had swiped from The Emporium. He would've fooled everybody if he had glued his ears back somehow, maybe with plugs of bubblegum.

Freddy said that Willie would've burned Dumbo in the hundred-yard dash. Instantly, a girl dressed in a white tutu loaded with rainbows of sequins, her cheeks plastered red with rouge, long hair rolled up in a tight bun, began waving her wand in Sister Ann's face. It was Cindy. The only thing that in any way disguised her was a mask like The Lone Ranger's that had been painted silver with a million rhinestones glued on it. No matter what question Sister asked, Cindy's was always the first hand to go up fluttering like a wiper at top speed. "It's Willie!" she exclaimed. "Cindy putita," The Mummy in the back moaned. He had rags plastered all over his body, and slime was oozing from both armpits. Willie headed back dejectedly down the aisle. "Putitoooo," said The Mummy. "What did you say?" Sister Ann demanded. "Uh, I was praying I would win the contest, Sister," The Mummy replied as he clasped his bandaged hands together and mumbled, "Jesus, Mary, and Joseph" clearly enough for Sister to hear.

Sister called for the next contestant, and Cindy waved her hand frantically and then pranced up to the front. "It's Arturo!" exclaimed The Mummy. Arturo turned around to slug The Mummy, and Sister, thinking he had raised his hand to volunteer, called on him. "It's Cindy," said Arturo, trapped. Cindy slumped back to her seat disgustedly.

Next was María Martínez, who could've easily beat the shit out of Haystack Calhoun, her favorite wrestler. She was dressed in an old zoot suit her father must've made his First Communion in, complete with tie, a hat with a long feather, and a large looped chain that dangled all the way to her size-thirteen calkos. She had on a pair of old shades and for some reason—I guess as an added disguise—an Abraham Lincoln beard. If old Abe had been a pachuco, that's exactly how he would've looked.

María had the biggest of crushes on Arturo. "Any guesses?" Sister asked. "Arturo?" said The Mummy, innocently. María lowered her shades and glared at him. "Arturo?" inquired Sister, trying to look as innocent as possible. Everybody knew it was María, but nobody was willing to pay the price of revealing her identity. She could kill you if she got you in a bear hug and crushed your ribs, or just by holding you and letting her bad breath melt you into jack cheese. "Now who could this be?" chanted Sister Ann, thumbing her rosary at about sixty beads a minute. "Who wants to take a guess?" Sister Ann went on, her rosary now flying through her fingers at about one hundred and twenty beads a minute. The Mummy jabbed a pencil into Arturo's ass. "Arrrghh!" Arturo screamed. "Oh, thank you," Sister cried out, relieved, and turned to look at Zorro. Arturo's eyes were as large as the clock on the wall behind Sister Ann.

María Martínez was glaring hard at Arturo. If she cornered him after school for betraying her, their wondrous love, he wasn't gonna be able to say "trick or treat," much less go out with us to scour the neighborhoods come nightfall. "Yes?" Sister said, the beads zipping at one hundred and eighty per minute through her thin, elegant fingers, Christ on the Cross hanging on, getting dizzy, nauseated, ready to tirar tripas all over her black Sister-of-Charity-issue chinelas. María had folded her arms and was tapping her foot impatiently, daring Arturo, her querido, her very reason for living—or at least for coming to school day after day—to utter even a syllable of her name. "Young man?" Sister asked. Actually, it was as close to begging as a nun could get. The next step would be selling her soul, if not her body, to the devil. If she flipped through the beads any faster she was going to send Christ crucified flying across the room and into the bulletin board, into the universe of gold stars aligned after Cindy's name. "María," Arturo said, and María stomped back to her seat, snorting. The score was Arturo two, Cindy one. "Arturo's a lambe," teased The Mummy.

Up next walked a boy in a homemade Superman outfit, complete with red cape. He was wearing shoulder pads over a tight blue sweatshirt and a pair of gym trunks over a dyed pair of long johns. He had plastered his hair with pomade and his face was hidden behind a plastic mask. When he walked, it sounded like he was wearing flippers. It was Froggie, no doubt about it. Cindy was waving her hand desperately in Sister's face, and Sister, feeling the need to move faster and lay the party to rest, called on her. "It's José!" Cindy squealed, and Sister put another check next to her name.

Then it was Sapo's turn. He waddled to the front encased in three large snowballs, an old derby perched rakishly on top, a corn-cob pipe stuck in his mouth. He had a bright red scarf wrapped once around his neck, the long end trailing behind him, and was carrying a janitor's broom. It must've been a million degrees inside that outfit. On a normal day Sapo's shirt would be stained with huge half-moons under both arms. Already the stains were grow-ing, waxing to full buttery yellow moons over the middle snow-ball. Cindy was squirming with excitement, her hand waving like she was a short-tempered cop directing traffic. Sister had to let somebody else guess just to make it look fair, so she called on María, who guessed correctly. Sapo struggled back to his seat and The Mummy planted his foot on the scarf, sending Sapo crashing into Arturo.

Sapo was followed by Pluto, who was wearing a suit, no tie, his shirt unbuttoned to his navel. He had a guitar slung over his shoul-der, and his hair was slicked back and high, a huge pompadour. No mask, just some sideburns and a pair of dark shades. "It's Toneee!" exclaimed Cindy, not even waiting to be asked. Sister waved Pluto back to his seat, but he had already plugged in the microphone. He had hauled the speakers in during the noon hour, and it was evi-dent he hadn't gone through all that trouble for nothing. He strummed the guitar, shook his hips, and began "Weeeelll, you ain't nuthin' but a hound dog—" "Anthony, please sit down!" Sister implored. "When I said you was high-claaassed . . . well, that was just a lie." "Anthony, please go to your—" "Well, you ain't never caught a rabbit and you ain't no frrriend of miiine!"

It finally occurred to Sister that pleading was not gonna do it, so she began applauding, encouraging us to join in. She clapped as hard and as loud as she could. "Weeell, you ain't nuthin' but a hooouuud dooog . . ." Sister urged us on until we drowned Pluto out and he disconnected the microphone and strolled back to his seat proudly, as if he had just wowed the nation on the Ed Sullivan Show. "Pludo ain't nudin' but a pudooo," The Mummy chanted.

Then came Angie as Snow White in a beautiful dress like a wedding gown, long white gloves, fancy white bows everywhere, a plastic Snow White mask. Sister gave Sapo a chance to guess, and he guessed right. Huge yellow moons were dripping down the middle snowball.

Cindy raised both hands as The Mummy came trudging up the aisle, ketchup and mud smeared all over his cloth bandages, slime oozing from his underarms and dripping onto the floor. His arms were flailing madly, out of control, slinging slime everywhere. "Freddy!" Cindy said as Sister pointed to her. The Mummy trudged back, caught an "apercut" in the groin from Arturo, and had to struggle to his seat, his monster walk for real now.

"Next," Sister said, running the show as quickly as possible, the end almost in sight. Up sauntered a sultry black cat. The Mummy was rubbing his crotch hard, though it was difficult to tell if it was because he was still in pain or because of Millie. "Millie!" The Mummy groaned. "Millie!" shouted Cindy and racked up another point. "Milliiie," The Mummy moaned, both hands working away at his groin.

Then an old woman struggled up the aisle. The Mummy's hand shot up, and he asked if he could go to the bathroom. He was squirming and pawing himself. Sister had a funny look on her face. She had to be asking herself the same question we were: Just how was this mummy going to unbutton himself quickly, etc., if he had to go so badly? She excused him and gave Pluto a chance, but he said it was Willie, and Sister reminded him Willie had already been up. María Martínez got another chance and added Victor to her list.

I volunteered to go next. Sapo and María stood up at the same time to get a better look and collided into each other. Sister called on Sapo, and he said "It's Johnny," and there went my chance for a prize.

Arturo walked up with a flair, cutting the air with his sword, whoosh whoosh whoosh, in the form of a Z. Cindy's hand was about to fly off her arm. Arturo had cut a piece of wig into a mustache and eyeholes into what looked like a very expensive scarf. I'm sure the next morning his mother turned the house upside down looking for it frantically before Mass. He was holding his cape up to hide his chin and mouth. All you could see was his mustache. Pluto shouted out "María!" Arturo shook his head. "Johnny!" Pluto shouted. Arturo shook his head vigorously. Sapo raised his hand and shouted "Raymundo!" Arturo shook his head and aimed his sword at Sapo. The Mummy had walked in, and María Martínez told Sister he'd said a dirty word. Sister told him to go back to the boys' bathroom and pray until the party was over. So The Mummy trudged out and enjoyed two more Pall Malls. Suddenly I raised my hand and Sister called on me, and I said "Arturo!" I finally had a point. (It wasn't until we were walking home after school and Arturo asked why I had identified him that I realized what I had done. It hadn't even occurred to me that I had ruined his chances of winning the prize. I had betrayed him and felt ridiculously stupid. I guess he realized it, because he dropped it and never brought it up again.)

Sister's thank-God-school's-almost-over! look flashed across her face. "Now who could this little devil be, God bless his soul," she cried out. Sapo and María were again wedged in the aisle as they struggled to come forward for a better look at the next contestant. Somehow Pluto, who had been combing his pompadour, had managed to get caught in between them. María shifted her hips, and Pluto let out a whoosh like a broken accordion, and Sapo crushed Pluto's guitar. The strings snapped with a loud twank. The Mummy had just returned, and Arturo had stuck his foot out, sending him crashing into María, who trapped him in her famous bear hug. "You give?" she asked. "Children, pleeeeze!" cried Sister Ann. Cindy let out a shriek, and if it hadn't been a Catholic school the windows would have easily shattered. "Give?" María asked again, breathing hard into The Mummy's face. "Farrggh you," said The Mummy. Slime was squirting from his underarms, and suddenly, as María squeezed harder, a stream of The Mummy's lunch flew out of his mouth and headed straight for Pluto's hair. "Pleeeze," said Sister Ann as she headed down the aisle. "Freddy puto!" Pluto said, and caught The Mummy with a right to the head. The Mummy yelled "Farrrggghh!" and kicked Pluto in the groin. María held onto The Mummy with her right and smacked Pluto into Sister Ann with her left. Pluto stepped on his guitar (thrangthunk), and now he was wearing it like a shoe. He landed on top of Sister Ann, and Sister cried out, "Oh my God!" which is what Pluto and Freddy, who were both a year older than we were, said the girls always shouted once they let you get on top of them. "Give up?" María asked again, getting ready to squeeze even harder. "Faaarrggh no!" The Mummy exclaimed. A glop of lunch gushed out and landed on Sapo. "Farrghh!" "Oh my God! Oh my God!" Waldo was aiming a hook at The Mummy when Arturo jumped in and connected with an "apercut." Sapo grabbed him in a ferocious headlock. "Give?" he asked. Arturo was drowning in the yellow moon under Sapo's arm. By now Cindy had gone for Sister Frances, the principal. "Give up?" María persisted. "Farrrggh" replied The Mummy. "Oh my God! Oh my God!" exclaimed Sister Ann. "Give?" Waldo asked Arturo. "Mmmmph," Arturo said. His arms were dangling, limp. I decided to jump in. I went to kick Sapo in the nuts and I slipped, either on The Mummy's slime or on his lunch or both, and then I saw María falling towards me.

When I came to I saw a huge figure standing over me, and I thought it was María falling on me again. I tried to cringe, but it took too much effort. Somebody was asking me if I was okay. Slowly, Sister Frances came into focus. The janitor was mopping up the last of the slime and puke, and Sister Ann was ordering the class in, threatening everybody there would be rosary after rosary after school if necessary. She asked if we were ready to act like grown-up boys and girls, and when we assured her we were she said we could continue with the party.

She called the little devil to the front, and Pluto said "Johnny!" and Sister said "no," looking at her pendant watch. "Remember," she said, "you have only thirty seconds to guess." "Hmm, is it Willie?" asked Millie. The little devil shook his head. Willie's hand went up, hesitantly. "It's Victor?" he asked. The little devil took his time replying, eating up time. "No." "Frog . . . , uh, José," said Victor. Again the little devil hesitated. "Time!" Sister Ann called out. She asked the devil to unmask.

It was Raymundo.

No wonder he hadn't brought lunch that day. He had gone home at noon and put on his costume there instead of changing with us in the boys' bathroom. Then he had walked back with the costume on so that nobody, not even us, would know it was him. Oh, the devil worked in mysterious ways!

Sister walked to her desk, pulled two envelopes out of a drawer. "The winner of the masquerade is Raymundo Martínez!" she declared. "He wins a rosary blessed by the archbishop." The class ooohed and aaahed. Pluto said he thought the prize was going to be one of Elvis's albums. Cindy was awarded the prize for most guesses. "It's a statue of Mary," Sister announced proudly. It was probably made in China by the Communists. Cindy was shriek-ing, "Thank you, Sister, thank you."

"Now that Raymundo has a new rosary," Sister said, "perhaps we can persuade him to lead us in prayer."

Raymundo nodded piously and began, "In the name of the Father . . ."

The Mummy fainted, or at least pretended to, after the First Sorrowful Mystery. Sister went with him to the door of the boys' bathroom, where he said he thought about us, our knees aching while he enjoyed a nice long smoke. ▪

We weren't even a block away from school, and already we had to stop and settle several questions and issues. First of all, we established a Time Out. Time Out was necessary in order for us to agree which words were considered cusswords and which were not. During a Time Out you could cuss as much as you wanted or needed to and it wouldn't count against you. And dur-ing a Time Out you could repeat all the cusswords everybody had used (if you could remember them all) in order to settle accounts. It took time to figure out who had said what and how many chin-gasos on the shoulder were owed to whom and by whom. Half a block later we established a new rule: We could call Time Out if (or better yet, when) we needed to in order to switch shoulders.

To begin with, Freddy was furious not only because we con-stantly got him for cussing, but also his Pall Malls had been crushed. He was forced to smoke bits and pieces no bigger than butts.

Then Arturo got angry because we slugged him for throwing a finger. "That's not cussing!" he argued. Freddy assured him that it was. Arturo, of course, told him he was full of shit, which provoked another outbreak about who said what and to whom and when and how many times. Raymundo asked Arturo which fingers he dipped in holy water to make the sign of the cross, and Arturo showed him, and then Raymundo asked him which he used to flip a finger, and—of course—Arturo told him he was full of shit, and then Freddy reminded Arturo he had said shit, and Arturo told Freddy he had said shit too, ask Johnny, and back and forth and on and on until we stopped and went through our calculations and tabulations.

In the end nothing was settled, because Freddy absolutely refused to believe any of Arturo's figures, and naturally Arturo thought any arithmetic Freddy did was certain to be wrong, and that's when I realized how to get back at Raymundo.

"Hey, Raymundo," I said, "you could've made a lot of money with this game, you know that? Imagine how much you would've made for being the inventor."

"With you guys, the way you cuss, I could have a Jaguar in no time."

"Let's see," I said, "how much could you make if you got a nickel a punch and collected from three people for three punches?"

He pretended to make a few calculations and then said, "Hey, a lot of bread."

"That's right, a lot." I persisted: "And would you make more or less if three people paid you ten cents a punch for ten punches?"

"Yeah," Arturo said. "How much would that be, man?"

"Shut up, Arturo," Raymundo said. "I'm thinking."

"I've figured it out already," Arturo proclaimed.

"Me too," Freddy said.

"Aw, bullshit," Raymundo told him.

"That's ten, you fucker!" Arturo yelled, pouncing on Raymundo at once.

"Shit!" Raymundo yelled.

"Ten, you asshole," Freddy joined in.

"And ten for you, Arturo, for saying fucker!"

"Ten more!" shouted Arturo triumphantly.

"Bullshit!"

"That's ten more for saying bullshit, man!"

"Hey, screw you, I didn't say bullshit!"

"Ten more. You did too say bullshit. Ask Johnny!"

"Screw Johnny!"

"Hey, man—that's ten more!" We pummeled him as hard as we could, and when he recuperated and wanted to get even, I said, "Hey, screw this game!"

"Yeah," Freddy said. "Screw this game!"

"Yeah," Arturo chimed in, "scareeeew this game!"

Freddy was craving a cigarette. "Pinche Arturo," he said, trying to empty his shirt pocket of any loose tobacco. There wasn't enough left for him to make a cigarette out of notebook paper. "You owe me a pack of Pall Malls, puto."

Arturo said, "You're as full of shit as your grandma's outhouse."

We walked the rest of the way to Raymundo's house in silence. We said "later" and didn't hang around to lift weights.

The rest of the way home it was "¡Cabrón!" and "¡Puto!" as Freddy swung at Arturo, and Arturo sidestepped him and kicked him in his fat ass, and "¡Jodido!" as Freddy kicked Arturo in the nuts, the three of us happy to be able to express ourselves as freely as possible as guaranteed by the Constitution.

(Fig) Newton, Bernoulli, and the Pink (and Green and Yellow and Even Blue) Elephants

One morning, after a thousand cases of Budweiser, Antonio Figueroa gave up drinking. "Elephants," he said, "pink and green and yellow elephants. I ain't never gonna drink again." Then he tumbled back onto the seat of the one-eyed Ford, or where the backseat used to be before he set it on fire. (Fig was a chain-smoker, too—Pall Malls.) His head hit the bumper we had lost the night before on the way to Miami (New Mexico), the Home of the State Reformatory for Boys and site of the biggest rodeo of the summer. Then he was snoring, and then I heard the trumpeting of elephants. No, I thought, it couldn't be, and lifted my head just far enough to peek over the dashboard, and sure enough: eight elephants, running down to the Miami River on a lazy summer morning: pink and green and yellow and even blue. But let me begin where I should, at the beginning. ▪

There was only a handful of jobs in San Miguel after the mines closed. The few that seemed up for grabs were available only if you were a Martínez or a close relative of a Martínez. After high school Fig and I hung around La Golondrina for a while to pass away the mornings. In the afternoons we shot baskets in my backyard. When evening came, you'd find us down by the river practicing our bull riding. We had tied an old barrel to four cottonwoods, and we rode and got throwed by lantern light far into the night. When we heard the railroad was hiring out by the Navajo Reservation, Fig and I hitchhiked west, where we landed a job on a repair crew working alongside Kee Begay—who, it turned out, was a bull rider just like us.

We had to lie about our age, but Fig was such a good talker he got himself hired easily, and once he learned that the hiring clerk's wife was from San Miguel, Fig asked him how his wife was going to treat him knowing he didn't hire the guy who scored thirty-five points in the triple overtime state-championship victory over the Miami Eagles. "That there's Johnny Barros," he said, introducing me, and the clerk said, "You got yourself a job if you want it, Johnny."

Before long we had learned a few words in Navajo. After a month or so the three of us pooled our money and bought a car, an old Ford, for a hundred dollars. Once we had a few dollars to spare, we decided to pool our cash and make money at what we did best: riding bulls. Not only would we make money, but we would also get ourselves a championship buckle and any girl we wanted. Once we started winning, we would get enough money together that the three of us could ride each weekend instead of having to take turns.

We had worked out a system: one weekend we'd sponsor Kee in one of the Indian rodeos on the nearby reservation. The next, Fig or I would try our luck in any rodeo the old one-eyed Ford could get us to and return us from in time for the six o'clock whistle Monday morning.

One thing I could never figure out was how Kee always ended up with the prettiest girls whenever we went to the rodeo dances on the reservation. ■

Little by little Fig and I began picking up some mannerisms of the Navajos, the Dinéh. You never touched an older man, even (or especially) in a friendly way. Handshakes were not hard or firm, vigorous. You ate bread by holding it in your left hand and tearing off pieces with your right. And most importantly, the first thing one Navajo asked another was what clan he or she belonged to. (Fig and I belonged to the Nakai Dinéh—"the Mexican People Clan.") ■

As soon as the foreman yelled "quittin' time!" that blistering day in August, we threw our picks and sledgehammers into the cart, rode back to the office, picked up our checks, and headed for Pete's Bar, where we bought five cases of Bud, put in a tankful of gas, and filled up the two five-gallon water cans we carried because of the leak in the radiator.

They always had the toughest, meanest bulls at the Miami rodeo. They also spared no expense when it came to championship belt buckles, which were usually presented to one of the "graduates" of the nearby reform school. And the prize money was tops, too.

We were anxious to get there early enough for the big dance. I was anxious to see Elsie. Buck Owens was gonna play, and I was hoping I would find her, but if I didn't, well, there would be plenty of girls everywhere you turned.

Fig promised—no, guaranteed—that come Monday morning one of us would be wearing that huge buckle with CHAMPION— BULL RIDING—MIAMI RODEO engraved on it. He had been working on—no, refining—his calculations all summer, and all we had to do in Miami was measure the bulls and pick up the buckle. That's how sure he was about applying Bernoulli's Principle to the gentlemanly sport (no, art) of bull riding.

Fig had fished out a six-pack, handed me and Kee a beer, and had guzzled one down by the time I had opened mine and put it to my lips. He lit a Pall Mall and set it in the right-hand corner of his mouth, where it would stay until it was too short to puff on and just long enough for him to spit out. Meanwhile, the ashes fell and burned more and more little holes in his shirt and Wranglers.

I had the Ford up to about forty, top speed, when he started in. "You see, guys, bull riding is very simple. Very simple indeed." He had already downed another Bud and didn't show any signs of slowing down. Sure, I thought. That's why we're so loaded down with championship buckles. I caught a glance of Kee in the rearview mirror, steeling himself for another long lecture on the physics of bull riding. "You see, it all boils down to physics." Fig had been an A student in math all through high school. He had been named

Fig Newton in our senior year when he excelled in Newton and physics. "Now the bulls know that Linear Velocity equals Angular Velocity times the Radius of the Circle. They know that. Shit, if the bulls could talk they would go so far as to tell you that this is a consequence of Newton's Second Law." "Oooh, bullshit," Kee moaned. "That's why the second the chute is opened," Fig continued, as if he had never been interrupted, "they begin to spin like shit in a hurricane." I felt it my duty to tell him a bull did it out of instinct. "I'm a burro when it comes to math," I said, "but I know a bull doesn't know any more about physics than I do." "But that's exactly it, Johnny," Fig countered. "He doesn't know more than we do. And that's why we're gonna outsmart him."

By now the Pall Mall had burned down, and he spat it out the window and quickly lit another as he grabbed another Bud. The old Ford was beginning to heat up, so I slowed down to twenty-five. We would get another twenty miles or so down the road before we would have to stop and put some water in the old Ford and let some out of young Fig.

"What I want to know," I said, "is how our pal Kee back there manages to get all the pretty Navajo girls all the time." It seemed to me that even though a girl showed interest in Fig or me, the next thing you knew she was being escorted away by Kee.

"I have it all figured out," Fig said.

"Great," I answered, "because it's really got me puzzled."

"Tonight or tomorrow morning," Fig went on, "we have to step into the corrals and measure every single bull."

"Bullshit!" I said, realizing he was still talking physics.

"Oh, there will be plenty of that," Fig continued, "but my whole theory depends on measuring each and every bull. So you have to step on a little bullshit to win a buckle. Sometimes in life you have to plow through it, sometimes you can sidestep it, but not this time. Now we're going to look stupid, so that's why I suggest doing it at night. Believe me, if those other dudes knew what we know, they'd be willing to wallow in bullshit up to their butts." He fished out another Bud.

"I'm telling you guys, this is a sure thing," Fig went on. "Now you take a bull that's five feet long and weighs eighteen hundred pounds. Now that's a lot different from a bull that's six feet long and weighs a ton. First size, then speed has to be taken into consideration. Is the bull fast or slow, we ask ourselves. And just how do we determine speed?" Fig questioned us. "Simple," he said, answering himself as he pulled out a stopwatch. "What we have to do besides measure them is check how fast they spin—how many revolutions per minute. We know Linear Velocity = Angular Velocity × the Radius of the Circle. What we have to do now is this: apply force to overcome the angular momentum. Angular Momentum = Mass × Radius × Velocity. Momentum = Mass × Velocity. To overcome momentum we have to apply force in the opposite direction so that the two cancel each other out. If we measure the bulls and know where to tie the rope so that we can lean without being thrown, once we know size and revolutions per minute we can leave Miami with a championship buckle on our belts, lipstick on our collars, and who knows—maybe even two headlights on the old one-eyed Ford, maybe even a new radiator."

"I don't know," I said. "Those bulls those guys raise up at the reformatory are pretty mean. I've heard they feed them chile pequín and locoweed, especially at rodeo time."

"I might even patent this gimmick. Start up a damn school like Jim Shoulders in Oklahoma," Fig said. "We'll teach those young cowboys physics in the classroom and bull riding in the corrals." He had finished his Bud.

I couldn't get another yard out of the old Ford, so I announced I had to stop to let it cool down.

"Perfect timing," Fig said. "I was just going to ask you to pull over."

"The only thing I know that leaks more than you is that old radiator attached to this pile of metal we call a car," I told him.

Fig scooted out of the car, squirming.

"Bernoulli's Principle: Force goes down as Velocity goes up. But in the end, it's really just another consequence of Newton's Law: Force = Mass × Acceleration," Fig said, beginning to look relieved.

"Yeah, yeah," I said. "Just finish taking your leak so we can get started. We gotta get to the dance."

We had been on the road for well over an hour and had traveled no more than thirty-five miles. We could still make the dance if we could cover the next eighty miles in two hours or so. It was simply a matter of Force = M × A.

I had filled the water cans at the gas station, but after doing so I had left them there and went to use the restroom, assuming that Fig or Kee would load them. They hadn't.

I had half a mind to leave the car and hitchhike into Miami. I didn't want to miss the dance, a chance to see Elsie. After waiting for half an hour and without a single car or truck passing, I was ready to try anything.

By now the sun had gone down. Fig must've sensed my impatience. He disappeared into the darkness, and the next thing I heard was cloth ripping on barbed wire and the irritated moaning and mooing of cattle, then shortly afterwards, the same ripping of cloth and then Fig huffing and puffing towards us, holding his battered Stetson like a ring bearer at a rich lawyer's wedding. But I had smelled him long before I had seen him.

I switched on the headlight because he wanted the hood raised, and then he carefully—oh, so carefully—tried to pour the precious water into the radiator. All he got for his efforts was a cloud of steam. "What I need," he said, "is another beer."

We decided the only way to get back on the road was to transport as much water as possible by any means possible. An hour or so later we had carried about a gallon in our hats and in beer cans and had poured all of it in, only to see it all evaporate. "Hey, no more pissing around," Fig said when he had to take another leak. Which he did. Right into the radiator.

We saw a pair of headlights approaching, but Fig was stuck between the strands of wire and we were at the water tank, too far from the fence to run and flag it down. The car whipped by so fast all we heard was the whinnying of the motor and then nothing but the chirping of the crickets and the slosh, slosh, slurp of our boots as the mud tried to suck us under.

When we got to the fence, Fig was still stuck. I stepped on the lower strand and pulled up on the middle so he could step through. "Hooke's Law," he said. "$F = KX$. It deals," he went on, "with such things as force applied, the inherent property of the wire, and the displacement. Another consequence of Newton's—"

I had seen a pair of headlights zipping down the highway and let go of the wires, running as fast as I could, waving my arms in desperation. I heard a loud "Aieeiee!" behind me.

I leaped out onto the middle of the road and flailed my arms frantically. The headlights drew closer, but there wasn't any sign the driver had seen me, no whining down of the motor. Whoever it was, he or she was doing at least seventy-five. At least. If I hadn't jumped out of the way, I would've been flattened, joining the remains of the skunks and raccoons and coyotes along Highway 88.

The pickup sped by, and about one hundred yards down the road the driver slammed on the brakes, ground the gears, and began backing toward us. He drove in reverse the same way he drove going forward. He hit the brakes when he was about ten feet away from the Ford, and the pickup skidded right into the grill.

Then there was the grinding of gears, the squeal of rubber as the pickup lurched forward. Fig had come into the light, barking instructions to the driver. Then the slamming of brakes, the crunching of gears, and the pickup backing up like a crazed elephant into the Ford again. "Perfect!" Fig shouted. He was caressing his fat butt with both hands.

Fig walked over to me and said, "This adds a whole new dimension to my calculations." He was going to have to ride favoring one nalga and he had to work out a new formula.

In the meantime out of the pickup stepped a figure that was at least six feet six, seven feet if you included the Stetson. The figure, which looked like an emaciated flagpole in the dark, was approaching us cautiously, a flashlight taped to his ready .30-30. He was shining the light in our faces, walking cautiously, cautiously, then suddenly he stiffened, sniffed the air like a famished timber wolf, and asked, "Now you boys ain't been smoking any of that 'mary-wanna,' have you?"

"Oh no, none of that," Fig assured him. "Just happened to step on a couple of cow pies, that's all."

The man took another whiff, a deep one, as he lowered the beam of the flashlight to our boots and then, finally convinced, clicked the rifle into safety and smiled.

The instant he stepped into the dull glow of the headlamp we recognized him: it was Red, the referee who worked all of Miami's home games, which would've been okay except that he was from Miami. He had glasses thick as the double soles on his boots and talked as if he had swallowed a referee's whistle. He had refereed the game the year before when we took (and I mean took) the State Football Championship. Miami had been state champs for as long as anybody could remember, but we had kicked their ass in basketball two years in a row. They were going to have a hard time shaking that off. And I wondered if Red knew that his beloved Miami Eagles smoked "marywanna" before their games. Those dudes were tough, man. Most, if not all, of them had been "recruited" from the state reformatory. Putting them in football uniforms was giving them a license to kill.

"You having car problems?" Red asked.

"Radiator," Fig said.

"Name's Red." He cradled the rifle in the crook of his left arm and extended his hand. "I was lucky enough to be born in Texas, but Miami's my home. We've been state champs in football for as long as anybody can recall. And any other sport you can think of. Basketball, baseball, track. And rasslin' too."

"We were on our way to Miami—gonna ride some bulls tomorrow," Fig told him.

"Why, shoot—I'll pull you three fellers and throw in a couple of beers along the way. You boys twenty-one, ain'cha?"

We nodded, earnestly, enthusiastically.

"Where you fellers from, anyway?" Red asked.

"San Miguel," Fig said, somewhat timidly.

"Now some folks would call this consortin' with the enemy," Red said, "but I got a code I live by. I've been refereein' games for twenty-five years now, and a man like me has got to be impartial.

Now the Eagles and the Rattlers is mortal enemies, but that's on the field. You boys follow me."

He hooked a chain around his hitch, latched the other end to our bumper, clanged his truck into first, and then peeled out, nearly yanking our bumper off.

Red flew right through Luna and had to make a U-turn at the end of the main street to get back to Casey's Bar. He ordered Buds for everybody at the bar. "I'm on my way back from a refereein' clinic in Las Cruces," he went on. "I like to keep up with the latest rule changes."

Fig nudged me with his elbow. This guy had missed an entire town and he was refereein' games?

"I've been refereein' games for twenty-five years now," Red said before putting the bottle to his lips, "and I've never made a call I couldn't live by."

Fig and I nearly fell off our bar stools. We were the only team ever to defeat Miami at home twice, and we wouldn't have won if Blue Moon Martínez hadn't switched Red's pistol and cartridges for one with a blank cartridge the first time, and we wouldn't have won the second championship if it hadn't been for Blue Moon Martínez stealing Red's flag on the last play of the game as Fig, our middle linebacker, tackled Miami's Benavidez on the two-yard line. Benavidez had run like an elephant on locoweed all night, and of course Red had been throwing his trusty flag against us at the right times. Blue Moon had been hit on the back of the head with a wine bottle tossed by one of the Eagles as we passed their huddle outside their locker room. Before the game they were passing a couple of joints and a bottle or two of cheap wine. You never got off the bus in Miami without your helmet on, even in your street clothes. It was a combat area. For Blue Moon, however, the blow on the head turned out to be just what we needed: he caught eighteen passes, three of them for touchdowns.

But if getting into the stadium was bad, getting out was worse, especially if you were taking the state championship trophy with you. We were pelted with beer cans, beer bottles, whiskey bottles, potato chips, cow chips, candy bars, purses, French fries, bananas, brassieres, rocks, apples, Stetsons, key rings, and anything else that wasn't nailed down. The bus was rocked, kicked, spat on, peed on. To make matters worse, Blue Moon pulled up the window, pulled down his pants, and mooned the Miami fans as he waved Red's flag victoriously. It took a platoon of state police cars to escort us safely, not just out of the stadium and not just to the county line, but all the way home to San Miguel.

Fig had downed his Bud easily. "We're gonna try our luck with the bulls tomorrow in Miami," he said, changing to a safer subject.

"Really?" Red replied. "Well then, you'll be glad to know that I've been chosen as one of the judges by the Miami Chamber of Commerce."

Fig downed his second Bud in one gulp, then said to Red, "It's good to know somebody with your reputation will be in charge out there tomorrow."

"I'll be out there to see that everybody gets a fair chance," Red told him reassuringly.

"That's all we can ask for," Fig said, trying very hard to sound convincing. "I take it you're a family man," Fig added, trying to get on Red's good side.

"You bet. A fine lady. Hasn't missed a home game in twenty-five years," Red said, and ordered one more Bud for the road.

Fig had to go to the restroom. "$F = M \times A$" he said as he stood up. "Also, Bernoulli's Principle at work."

We checked the chain and Red sped off, our heads snapping back every time he switched gears. I was getting seasick. Red was going close to seventy. I stuck my head out the window and heaved everything. Fig was steering comfortably, opening another Bud and lighting another Pall Mall.

We were going to be in Miami in no time at all. The dance would be about half over. I would dance, dance, dance with Elsie for about an hour and a half and then . . . Elsie! Elsie! Elsie!

About ten miles out of Los Brasos, Red rounded a sharp curve and we didn't. Red's lights disappeared quickly into the darkness. We got out to look for the bumper we had heard clanging all over the highway, and Fig disappeared into a clump of bushes to take a leak. "Here it is," he shouted.

We were about ten yards from a house, so we decided to push the Ford close enough to fill the radiator with the water hose.

"Watch Bernoulli's Principle at work," Fig said as he went to turn the water on.

We could hear someone singing inside the house, "Ooh, my Rose, my roooose of San Antoooone!" And then immediately afterwards, a voice a little like Scarlett O'Hara's: "And I could waltz across Texaaaas with yoooouuuuuu!"

Suddenly we heard a car crank up. From behind a hedge came crashing a state police car, siren wailing, lights flashing, and out jumped a cop who stood at least six feet five and weighing about two sixty, with a voice as deep as Johnny Cash with a bad sore throat. "Up against the wall, muthafucka, spread yer laigs and keep yer hands on top of the car," he roared. Kee and I obeyed instantly. "Hey, Your Honor," he thundered, "here's two of them!"

The Honorable Raymundo Martínez, Esq., was sitting in the passenger seat, livid but unflinching.

I wanted to tell him he had the wrong guys, but nothing came out except some dry "uhs" and groans.

"I'll teach you to moan and groan over His Honor's . . . uh, friend," the big fellow bellowed. "When I get through with you . . ."

Fig came walking up to the car with the hose. "Let's hose her quickly and get the hell out of here," he said. "There's more women waiting on us in Miami."

"Three of them!" the state cop growled.

Then somebody shouted "Aiiieeee!" and we turned and saw a man tumbling off the porch steps, boots and shirt clasped in his arms, pants wrapped around his ankles. It was Caruso.

"Four?!!" shouted the police officer as he drew his gun. "Your Honor, she's screwing the whole goddamned county!"

"Shut up, Jenkins!" His Honor shouted. "Rose is not that kind . . ."

Officer Jenkins fired a warning shot. "Stop, cobarday!" he shouted. "Okay, Sheriff Sánchez," he barked, "move in!"

Caruso was limping into the darkness of an alfalfa field.

"Stop, you coward!" the policeman shouted. He told us not to move and took off running towards the field, firing warning shots.

Suddenly all the lights in the house went on and out ran a woman in a skimpy nightie, yelling "Help! Help!" She had a face like an underfed schnauzer. It was hard to tell if she was yelling "Rape! Rape!" or "Ray! Ray!"

Suddenly Sheriff Sapo Sánchez came blazing out of the alfalfa field, siren blasting. Caruso had already fired up his tow truck and was rocketing in the opposite direction.

Sapo nearly ran over the state patrolman, then swerved into the stairs, nearly crushing Rose of San Antone. "Stop! Sapo, stop! ¡Idiota!" His Honor the Mayor roared. Sapo was now carving a figure eight into the front lawn.

Fig, who had been filling the radiator, suggested we get the hell out of there. I threw the bumper in, and Kee floored the gas. He made a wide semicircle over the lawn, nearly crashing into Sapo. He charged through the hedge like a crazed elephant, then hit the highway. Sapo blasted another hole in the hedge, whirled into another figure eight, and crashed into the state police car.

Once we were on our way, Fig pulled out a Pall Mall and suggested we have a Bud to settle our nerves. ▪

Miami was jumping, but we had missed the dance and there was no chance of finding Elsie even by Fig's calculations. The streets were crowded even at three A.M. There were banners and posters everywhere announcing the ANNUAL MIAMI RODEO, along with colorful posters of giant elephants in single file, tails entwined with trunks, calling everybody's attention to the CIRCUS! CIRCUS! CIRCUS!

Kee managed to get through the traffic jam and the couples dancing in the street. He drove past the rodeo grounds down to the river's edge. Fig had drunk most of the beer on the last leg to Miami and stayed up to finish what was left. Kee and I were too exhausted to keep up, so we checked in early. I went to sleep thinking of Elsie, hoping I would impress her the next day by staying on the biggest, meanest bull. ▪

Next morning, Fig gave up drinking. "Elephants!" he said, "pink and green and yellow elephants," and then he fell back, hit his head on the bumper, and was out, snoring deeply until long past noon. I figured he was better off if I never told him about the six garrulous elephants that were later captured and led back to their compound by their trainer, a thin, pop-eyed man with a neatly trimmed Van Dyke, and his assistant, a thin platinum blonde with eyes like a catfish. They were part of the circus that came to Miami every year during rodeo week. Somebody had mixed in some locoweed with the elephants' breakfast, and every cowboy in the state was attempting to throw his lasso around the green, blue, yellow, and pink elephants. ▪

We woke up, luckily, about half an hour before the bull riding began. We splashed some water on our faces and staggered over to the corral, where Fig managed to make a few rough calculations. He managed to stay on a bull named Dumbo, but Red claimed his free hand had touched so he was disqualified. Kee got flung from a bull named Speedy Gonzales, and I came out of the chute two bulls later and was thrown—or better yet, hurled—by a bull named—believe it or not—Elsie's Bull. On the way home, with Kee snoring soundly in the back, I asked Fig if he possibly had any idea how Kee kept getting the prettiest girls for himself.

"Sure do," he said. He spat out the last of his Pall Mall, then went on: "He's been telling the ones he doesn't want to mess around with he's from their clan, so they're forced to go with somebody else."

"No shit?" I said. I drove for awhile in silence, then asked, "And how did you figure that out?"

"Well," Fig said, "did I ever tell you the story of Newton and Bernoulli? For years and years Bernoulli worked on a problem. But he couldn't solve it. And, by the way, contrary to what people will tell you, Bernoulli was Swiss, not Italian. Swiss of Italian descent. Anyway, everybody in the world of mathematics knew Bernoulli was working on this particular problem. Everybody, that is, except for Newton. Well, every day Newton would go to the park to eat his lunch, and it just happened that his maid would wrap his lunch in a newspaper.

"One day he's unwrapping his lunch, and he happens to see an article about Bernoulli and the problem he's been working on for so long. So what does Newton do? Well, he figures it out and mails the answer to Bernoulli, who's pissed off for the rest of his goddammed life."

"And the moral of this story is?" I asked.

"And the moral of this story is that you or me or anybody else is not the center of the universe; nobody knows everything. It was Ellen Roanhorse who told me all about Kee. She's the girl we met at the Grants Rodeo, remember?"

Fig paused, spat out his last Pall Mall: "If you want the secrets of the universe explained far beyond Newton and Bernoulli, get yourself a good woman—one like Ellen. That's exactly what I'm gonna do. No more pissing around."

La Matanza

The San Miguel Tribune
July 5, 1972
**MILLION-DOLLAR HEIST AT
SAN MIGUEL DOWNS!**

In an uncanny replay of a heist film, *The Killing*, a horse was shot during yesterday's running of "The Willkie Martínez Handicap" while a man wearing a suit, hat, and tie, his face concealed by a clown mask, and wielding a shotgun, robbed the San Miguel Downs of an estimated million dollars in cash in untraceable bills.

Security officials at the track stated that the bandit gained entrance to the finance office during an altercation at the grandstand bar when security officers were kept busy subduing a professional wrestler during a ten-minute fracas. The wrestler, whose name was not revealed, is undergoing questioning to determine if his altercation with a disgruntled fan was part of a master plan to create chaos at the track and distract officials.

Clerks in the finance center said the bandit had them stuff the money into a military duffel bag and then ordered them to lie facedown on the floor. They added that they had no idea how he had not been spotted, walking through the crowd carrying such an awkward and obvious load.

In an exclusive interview with the *San Miguel Tribune*, Detective Gil García of the FBI stated that the way the bandit went about committing the robbery led him to believe he was certainly inspired by a film, *The Killing*, that was shown recently at the Eros Theater in downtown San Miguel.

According to Detective García, the film stars Sterling Hayden in the title role of an ex-con named Johnny Clay, who has just returned to society from prison and immediately masterminds the robbery of a racetrack. In the course of the film a horse is shot, and a professional wrestler is involved in a large fight in order to create chaos while the bandit, who wears a suit, coat, and tie and whose face is concealed behind a clown mask, orders the clerks to stuff the money into a duffel bag while holding a shotgun menacingly. Early in the film Johnny Clay recruits, in addition to a marksman, a corrupt police officer, a bartender at the track, and a teller who works at a ticket window. "The similarity of the M.O. is uncanny," stated Detective García.

According to official records, the Eros is owned and operated by Mr. J. K. Singh, a native of Bombay, India, who is said to be a passionate film buff. Singh has reportedly been under surveillance for showing films with anti-American themes.

Detective García also added that roadblocks have been set up statewide. "We are rounding up the usual suspects," he said. He noted that a special investigative squad had been formed. "We will not rest until this case is closed and the criminals are behind bars," he vowed.

– – – – – – – – – – – – – – –

MARY ANN

April 1st, 1972

Dear Johnny,

The time goes by so slowly, but you'll be home soon.

As I told you in my last letter, the more I think about *The Killing*, the more I like it. I think you'll agree with me when you see it again that it's an important film. It's not for everybody, but I'm sure it'll make you think about whether or not crime pays.

When you see Sterling Hayden, you will feel as if you *are* Johnny.

Only someone as smart as Johnny, and who knew the right kind of people and how much their talents were worth, could pull this kind of heist off. Of course he never let one guy know how much the other guy was getting.

J. K. is sending you a box of Swiss chocolate on account of you are getting out soon. He says it's the best chocolate in the world—bank on it!

He is proud that you are reading a lot and encourages you to do as much research as you can. Time is getting short, so study and prepare yourself for the future.

Now that you have a job in the library, you should take advantage of your resources—appreciate your interests. The economy has changed here since the track was built.

A lot of opportunities to make money: two dollars at a time or hitting it big for a million.

I'm betting that Macaroon will be the long shot in "The Willkie Martínez Handicap" come July Fourth!

I miss you!

Love, Mary Ann

--- -- --- -- --- -- --- -- --- -- --- -- --- -- --- -- ---

HIS HONOR, RAYMUNDO MARTÍNEZ, MAYOR OF SAN MIGUEL

Yeah, you brought good films to San Miguel, but the fact remains, some goddamned pachuco—oh, I know who he is, J. K., I know who he is—somehow got a very fancy goddamned idea from a certain film he saw in your theater. He got a pretty goddammed good idea about how to steal some big money, and now you're going to have to answer a hell of a lot of questions, J. K., a hell of a lot of questions. You may even fry as an accomplice. I hope you're aware of that.

Somebody shot a horse, J. K. My wife's horse, Macaroon! Shot Macaroon right out from under the jockey! In front of a grandstand full of people. It was a sure winner. It was in the bag, J. K. There was a lot of money—a lot of *big* money riding on that little horse. Now my wife's not only out of some money, she's also out of a goddamned good horse. She's gonna call out the dogs, J. K. Oh, she's gonna call out the goddamned dogs! I goddamn guarantee you some heads are going to roll!

All those rich tejanos got scared off, J. K., and that means we're gonna lose even more money. The rest of the tourist season has just been flushed down the can. The Emporium is gonna be empty, and my wife . . . I've got a new form of yoga I'm recommending to you, J. K.—practice bending over and kissing your ass goodbye, J. K.!

FREDDY

As soon as Cyclone gets the chotas involved, I'll slip away quickly from behind my window and open the door. You have to move fast, Johnny. Remember, it's the two-dollar window closest to the door, but I still have to leave the cage to open the door. If you don't slide in quickly, it'll snap shut tighter than a bear trap and that'll be the end of this fine masterpiece.

Once inside, move quickly—don't rush but move quickly, just like you are one of the employees, up the stairs and into the first door on your left—remember that. You've got to be a blur but not an obvious one. That's the locker room.

When you come out of the locker room with the mask on and the shotgun ready, you've got to move really fast into the corridor. By the seventh race there'll be a million dollars waiting for you. So, into the locker room, get the duffel bag out of Wimpy's locker, then out of there smoothly, about five, six steps. When you press the buzzer to the room where the bucks are, lean on the door so it'll open quickly. The guard will be immediately to your left. Take him out right away, and the rest is easy. He's a big panzón, Sapo's primo, very slow. You're the only one who can judge how long to stay in there. Have the thin bald guy empty the money. He's a real nervous guy, but not clumsy, and he'll empty the shelves in no time at all.

You've got five minutes at most after the chotas jump on Cyclone. Stuff the shotgun and the mask in the bag quickly, tie the bag, and throw it out the window gently—so it lands without bouncing and rolling too much. You've got to be a blur walking out, Johnny. I'll try and stall anybody trying to get in after they haul Cyclone away, but you've got to get the hell out of there and melt into the crowd quickly, in step with everybody instantly. If anybody notices you on your way down, take them out quickly, neatly, and move on. Melt into that crowd quickly, Johnny. Quickly.

What's most important, Johnny, is getting in. Slide in quickly once I open the door, or that's the end of this grand heist.

They're gonna know somebody let you in. It won't take them too long to figure out it was me. Johnny, landing this job was the biggest break I ever got. The track was the best thing that ever happened to this podunk town. I could work there the rest of my life and I'd be okay. Yeah, I gamble. You and I know that. But I don't ever owe more than I can make. I swear that's the truth, Johnny.

But you know me, Johnny. If the pot's big, then I'm in. I'll always take a shot at the big money. I've always wanted to roll the dice in Monaco. Maybe we could go together, Johnny? The dames, fine wines, great chow, the tables . . . ▪

POPEYE

One day we walked up on a bunch of Vietcong having a strategy meeting. The officer was standing up pointing to a large map, so we had a clear shot at him. We were just a regular recon unit, not a sniper team, so all we had was our M16s. We decided to dust the officer, figured that would be pretty demoralizing.

I blew his shit away, man. He was dead before he even heard the shot.

A couple of months or so later, the chopper came in to exfil my buddy who had five days left in Nam. We said goodby, and he headed off for the chopper. He took his steel pot off—something they told you never, never to do way back in basic training—and tossed it in.

He was pulling himself up when a VC up in the trees blew his head off.

When I got home I started drinking, and I haven't stopped since. I go to the VA hospital once a month for some pills. A few pills, a lost year, and a bucketful of nightmares—that's all I got to show for serving in Vietnam.

Yeah, I can make the shot. And then I'm gonna get lost somewhere, maybe Kuala Lumpur.

If they catch me, what can they get me for? As the dude in the movie said: "The most they can charge you with is shooting a horse out of season."

I mean, what the fuck can they do to me? Send me to Vietnam? ▪

RATÓN

I paid a few relatives. All over the county there were fender benders, dead batteries, stalled vehicles. Caruso was towing cars all day long. Sapo didn't get a coffee break until the seventh race was about to begin.

I called headquarters. Told them I was having problems with the radio. Just like you told me, Johnny. Then I turned the radio off. Then I drove around and got to the track just before the seventh race. Then I parked under the window. Then I grabbed the bag. Then I stuffed it in the trunk. Then I turned the siren on. Then I drove out the main gate.

Sapo doesn't suspect a thing. But the mayor and his wife lost a lot of money. They're going to stop at nothing to get it back. They're going to spend a lot of money to get their money back. But by the time they do we'll all be long gone.

I've made more money off this than I made my entire life. My entire life working for idiotas like Sapo Sánchez. The mayor and his wife can squeeze my nuts all they want. But I won't talk. ▪

WIMPY THE BARTENDER

The shotgun will be in my locker, loaded, along with the gloves, the mask, and the duffel bag. I'll give Benavidez the signal to start in on Cyclone as soon as the horse goes down. He's gonna be pissed when he finds out he wasn't in on the big money, but fuck him. He's getting more than he's worth just for running his mouth and starting a fight, something he usually does for free. ▪

FACT

Sometime in the '60s, a group of men in Bombay held up a bank. The holdup followed the exact details of the robbery as depicted in *Highway 303*, a film that was playing at a downtown theater at the time. ▪

J. K. SINGH

It was a shame to see somebody like Johnny "go up," as they say here, to the state pen. Boy, I loved to watch him play football and basketball. He was great—especially against the Eagles of Miami! And he could ride a bull, too! I "lost track" of him, as they say here, after he went to work on the railroad out there by the Navajo reservation.

Next thing I knew, he was on his way to Vietnam. He drank a lot when he came home. A lot. One night he told me a story— about how a long column of VCs passed right next to them and how his recon team had to walk point for what is called a "line unit"—a company of infantry. He said that in the middle of the firefight the VC put a newborn baby up on the bunker. The Americans held their fire and were getting cut to pieces. Johnny said the guy who blew up the bunker was from New Mexico. They had to kill the baby to save their own lives, but at what price?

For Johnny the cost was heavy. He was getting medications from the VA hospital, and he was drinking them down with alcohol—beer, whiskey, whatever. One night he picked up a brick, flung it through the front window of The Emporium, slipped in, and stole some liquor. He had the shakes and had been hearing voices. His Honor the Mayor used every political connection he had to get Johnny sent to the State Pen up in Santa Fe for four years, a year for each bottle.

He was a bright kid, real bright. He didn't waste his time serving out those four years. He did a lot of reading: poetry, philosophy, history. I'm sure he also got a good education of the other sort. Not petty stuff, either. Big stuff. Like Swiss bank accounts and how to make money in the international market. He looked ahead, worked it so he got a job in the library with the big-money cons.

Oh, he loved film. Appreciated it. I show films because I love them; I, too, appreciate them. I wanted to show the best films I

And on All Your Children

It was an infant, wailing.

But the story begins in the morning, that monsoon morning, waking up soaked, with the dishpan hands of an overworked housewife, dishpan feet, too. Cookie, the radio man, pulls a pair of dry socks out of a plastic bag—as if they were going to keep his feet dry the rest of the day. In ten minutes they'll be as soaked as the ones he had on. But it's gotta help to at least go through the motions. And to actually have your feet nice and warm and hugged by a pair of calf-length, government-issue, olive-drab socks. I'm not that type, though. Just taking my socks off and wringing them, wriggling some life back into my toes, is enough. The damn rain won't stop. Didn't stop all night.

Rooks is on the radio from relay mountain asking for dry socks. "What does he need dry socks for?" asks Sergeant Gooch incredulously. "He's in a warm shack up on relay mountain manning the radio."

Gooch is a stateside GI. Knows nothing but Rules & Regs, barracks inspections, shit like that. He's gonna get us all killed out here in the boonies. Dumb motherfucking five-sided square. *Dry socks* is the code word for pot. When the supply chopper pays a visit today, Rooks, who's been up there a week already, will get a nice little package from Puckett, the cook. Inside a pair of dry socks.

An infant wailing for its mother's breast.

Sarge and his assistant—another fucking asshole, a buck sergeant who's into Rules & Regs (that's why Gooch chose him)—check and recheck their maps and chart our course for the day. The last time we were out in the bush, the dickheads had us walk about seven clicks in one day. This is a recon team, motherfuckers. We're supposed to observe the enemy's movements. Underline

the word *observe*. Cookie got a call asking if that was us moving so
fast. They not only have a gadget on choppers that can detect large
amounts of urine, tell you exactly where ole Charley Cong's been
camping out, but they also have a sensor that picks up movement.
We came pretty close to getting a shitload of artillery dumped
right on top of us. Stupid fucks.

We down a quick breakfast of LRRPs. With cold water. You
can't heat anything up out here. Charley will get a whiff of that
butane burning and blow your shit clear back to Nantucket. Don't
even think of slapping on aftershave before coming out here. Especially with only five other dudes besides you. And two of those
being dumb stateside fucks. And one of those being a Wallace sup-
porter from Alabama—that's Cookie. Now there's one dumb fuck,
alright. Threw himself on a grenade trying to win the Congres-
sional. But the damned thing didn't go off. It was a dud! So they
gave him a Silver Star and a special R&R to Hong Kong instead.
This is the dude who every time he was on guard duty back in
base camp when we were brand new in-country cherries claimed
he saw gooks charging the perimeter. We would grab our gear and
weapons and wait and wait—for nothing. The same dude who
one time in an infil signaled he had seen some gooks and crouched
down quickly in the tall grass and nearly got a punji stake right in
the balls. He got a Purple Heart out of that. Along with a speech
from some dry Major who said the same thing to all the other GIs
as he went from bed to bed, congratulating them all for their service and sacrifice; their country was proud of them.

But what's left for a southern boy nowadays? I mean you can't
secede and have another Civil War. So you go squirrel hunting—
on the other side of the big charco, as the World War II vets say.

And then there's Williams. Hard to tell about him. Goes around
telling everybody he can't stand the silence out in the boonies—
not being able to talk, communicating only by signals for days at
a time. Well shit, you can whisper out here, but I guess that's not
quite the same. You have to be listening all the goddamned time,
be on the lookout constantly. If you're the type that's gotta be running his mouth all the goddamned time, this shit out here will

drive you crazy. I mean, you can catch yourself singing (silently, of course) shit like "Twinkle, Twinkle, Little Star" out here, and maybe even "Mary Had a Little Lamb." Sometimes you can spend the whole day out here looking, looking for Charley, waiting, waiting, and your mind will wander. It will definitely wander. The monsoon season is the worst, because you can't hear Charley— the snap of twigs or the crackle of dry leaves. Of course he can't hear you either. That's what it's like with Williams. You don't know whether you're ahead of him or he's ahead of you. Anyway, I was talking about breakfast. You can have it three ways out here. With rainwater, if that's your preference. Or with rainwater with your purifying tabs thrown in. Or, if you're inclined, you can have it with regular water. One good thing about monsoon is you don't run out of water. You can catch the runoff from a leaf and have a fresh—I repeat, fresh—canteenful in no time at all.

We fold up our LRRP packets and stuff them in our packs. You don't bury anything out here and leave Charley traces of your visit. We roll up our poncho liners (some guys carry a poncho, but that makes your load bulky and you can't get too comfortable out here), check our weapons (it's good to apply a fresh coat of oil), and saddle up. In less than ten minutes the straps are digging into your shoulders. In this rain we could pass for a small pack of loaded-down burros climbing, tripping, sliding up and down hills and mountains. A pack of pinche burros. That's what we are. Who else would be out here slogging through this rain and mud but a goddamn burro?

Williams is walking point. Paranoids make good point men 'cause they're overly careful, but I'm just not sure about this guy. Is he saying all this stuff so everybody'll think he's crazy and not want to go out with him, thinking he'll get sent to a shrink and get shipped back to the world? I mean, if you were going nuts would you be sharing your deepest and darkest thoughts so publicly? Practically broadcasting them? On the other hand, wouldn't that be a perfect sign of madness? Goddammit, if he plays his cards right he'll have the U.S. Army snookered and be on that freedom bird (back to Birmingham) before me, and I'm at least six months shorter than he is. Ain't that a bitch? Making him walk point will keep him honest. If he fucks up, Charley will blow his shit away.

Then there's Sarge. If this was a line outfit, he would've been fragged a long time ago. Dusted. And the assistant squad leader, García. He's a Chicano from LA, a dry, stingy dude. Not much to say about him, because there's not much to him. Except that he's engaged. Even has the wedding date set (the very week he gets home from Nam). That's probably why he's so lifeless. He's scared to death. I hope (for his sake) he makes the army a career, because I don't know how else he's gonna be able to put some food on the table.

And me. I walk drag. Bring up the rear. The opposite of point. Except that while you're brushing grass back into place, you've also got to be watching out for Charley. Meanwhile, your back is turned and your squad is moving away from you—and perhaps into something. So you're cleaning up, like the guy behind the horses in the Fourth of July parade. If you tarry too long, you get left behind and break up the flow. Too little and you're bumping into traffic in front of you. It's an art, I tell you. One hand holding the weapon, thumb on the safety ready to flick it on Rock 'n Roll—full automatic at the slightest sound or movement—looking for Charley while at the same time looking to see if you've cleaned up well with your free hand, meanwhile glancing behind you to see what twists and turns the rest of the fellas have taken.

An infant, naked and screaming, and soft and loved like no other.

Last night I tried what the old sergeant in Recondo School advised we could do in monsoon if we got cold: piss in our pants. Yeah, you get warm. For about five minutes, maybe. Then it's back to cold again. And now I smell like piss. You'd think the rain would wash the smell off, but it doesn't.

I had an uncle I called Uncle Hoople (because he looked just like Major Hoople, the comic-strip character). Hrrumphed and talked big just like the major. He and only he knew how to cure the world's ills: los juvenile delinquents, increasing taxes, and the crooked politicians down at City Hall who never got around to having the potholes in the roads on our side of town repaired.

Uncle Hoople would stop by every morning after his shift in the mine to check on Grandma and Grandpa. I was living with my grandparents because my parents were divorced. I could hear Uncle Hoople roaring in the kitchen ("¡SONAMABISQUETE!")—complaining about the high cost of living or the inefficiency of our blundering sheriff, that's why the world was going to the dogs ("¡SONAMABISQUETE!")—and I'd wake up and immediately check to see if I was wet.

I was.

I'd swear I would stay in bed until Uncle Hoople left. Till noon. Sundown, if necessary.

But sooner or later I had to get up. Had to. Couldn't stand the smell. Or being soaked. Nothing left but to face Uncle Hoople.

His first words would be, "¿Cómo hace el gatito?" quickly followed by taunts of "meow, mea'o."

Every morning.

An infant wailing. Or was it the shriek of a man, unbelieving?

All morning we worked our way up and down mountains, pulling ourselves up by grabbing trees, an outstretched hand, or a rifle sling and making our way down by sliding voluntarily, involuntarily, holding on to trees, roots, rocks. And for what?

You can't see shit out here in monsoon. Do these assholes really expect you to observe troop movements? Find a new bunker complex? A large-weapons cache? All you can think about is sitting down and enduring the rain until the chopper comes to exfil us. There's fog in addition to rain out here. You'll see Charley only if he runs into you. I saw four or five trees that had been whacked by a machete, all of them at about what would be shoulder high for Charley Cong. No more than a day old. Trail markings. Freshly cut—still white—not even beginning to turn yellow. We're gonna get dusted, man. But you can't tell these spit-shine soldiers a goddamned thing. It isn't in the Rules & Regs, so they don't want to hear it. Okay, motherfuckers. But you just wait and see. Charley is going to hand us our ass. Up close and personal.

Let's see.
Are we following orders?
Are we following a trail?
Are we following a trail following orders?
And is Charley following orders?
Is Charley following his own trail?
Is he following his own trail following orders?
OR
Is Charley following us following him?
Twinkle, twinkle little star.
Chinga'o, goddamn, and fuck it!
An infant. Nameless. Beloved of God. His. And ours.
We're in a circle, facing outward, in, of all places, an open field. Why we've stopped, why this has been chosen as an observation post, I don't know. Must be a new tactic they're teaching at the NCO Academy these days. We're wearing camouflage fatigues and have camouflage stick all over our faces and hands so nobody can see us. We've cut irregular patterns of green tape and plastered them all over our weapons. We blend in perfectly with our surroundings. Not even Charley can find us, and we're right in his own backyard! Man, we're gonna get our ass handed to us.

The sarge signals for a lunch break. I stand up to remove my pack, and I see the flashes of the muzzles and fall back down. (Later, Cookie will tell me he thought I had been shot.) (Later, much, much later, I will continue to wonder what the hell happened. Did Charley fire too hurriedly? Obviously, it just wasn't my time to go. There's no explaining it.)

If we're not surrounded already, we will be soon. Son of a bitch! So this is where it ends. (Later, I will remember that I didn't have time to think of my entire life flashing before me, as the heroes in films and novels say. No, just enough to realize that this isn't really the way you imagined it would end; time only to say goodbye, but not to everything—you notice the trees, the sky, briefly, this may be the last you see of this earth you've lived on for nineteen and one-half years—and to everybody—parents, sisters, and brothers, yes, very quickly, but not to the crazy aunts, greedy uncles, old loves, the children you never had with that girl you secretly loved in third-period English, the women you dreamed about out here.) All the while you've flicked your weapon to full auto, scanning your slice of the horizon (hoping the rest of these motherfuckers are ever so vigilant about theirs). Something about laying down your life, a short phrase from the Bible or some sermon or catechism lesson, runs through your head. Scanning. Scanning. You are going to die. Soon. You've accepted that. You are going to die. At the least the odds are very high. And with no time to make your peace with the world. Only with yourself. And much too quickly to do you much good.

We wait. We are going to die. The one thing I fear is what happened to Jimmy. His team got surrounded and Charley dusted all of them except for him. Somehow he stayed alive until the choppers came and exfilled him. Sometimes you can't help but wonder if the guy wouldn't have been better off if they'd dusted him too. He walked around the company area, green eyes shattered, a ghost, haunted. Nothing anybody would ever say or do would help piece him back together again. How do you award somebody his life back, Mr. President?

We wait.

But Charley must be waiting, too. Waiting for us to make the first move.

Or, for some reason or another, he's gotten the hell out of here. Proof, then, this area is hot. If we get into a big firefight, he knows we'll call in air support. But then why did he open fire on us? He could've bushwhacked us if he had had just a little more patience. Maybe Charley's got some NCOs that are at least as stupid as ours. I doubt it, but you never know.

I pass the word on to Sarge. We need to didi mau—get the hell out of here fast. He thinks about it. We need to break out if Charley's trying to surround us. If he's waiting for reinforcements, we're helping him if we don't make a move to get out. There's no way a chopper could get in here to exfil us. Too many tall trees too close together. We better didi, carefully but fast, and find an LZ.

We begin to file our way north, away from where the shots came, as quickly as possible, staying as low as possible, crawling, slinking away as low as possible on all fours like hungry foxes raiding the chicken coop, knowing that one slipup and it's the farmer coming out with his shotgun, blasting away.

I'm a short-timer. Nine days and a wake-up to go. I carry three bandoleers. Two across my chest, Zapatista-style, and one around my waist (in addition to the two magazines, one in the weapon and the other taped upside down to it, ready to turn and jam in quickly). Everybody else carries two. I have a slipknot on the bandoleer around my waist. We get into any shit with Charley and I can lay it in front of me quickly, ready to pull out one magazine right after the other quickly, lay as much fire down as I need to. I'm short, man. I haven't come this far to let Charley get into my shit now. Nine goddamn days and a wake-up.

We crawl and stumble until we're pretty sure we're safe. And then we wait. And then we crawl away again. And wait. Wait.

Nothing.

We have been spared. (For whatever reason we have been spared.)

There is no other word for it.

It's a miracle. (A motherfucking, goddamn miracle!)

There's no greater miracle than having your life—your life granted back to you. Oh, if you could learn to live each day like that moment you promised, promised, swore that you would never, never take it for granted ever, ever again! (A dude who had spent a year down in the Delta had this engraved on his Zippo: "YOU'VE NEVER REALLY LIVED UNTIL YOU'VE ALMOST DIED.") You have been allowed to be born again. Only the evil and the damned know the joyous chant of resurrection.

An infant.

No, clearly there is no greater miracle than a newborn infant. An infant is you all over again (but, of course, not you) played out in front of you to love and worship and guide and inspire and dream for and change the world for.

We're able to make another click before the rain begins to come down hard, mercilessly. We can't be too far from the LZ where we'll be exfilled tomorrow. One more goddamned night out here. I'm short, man, getting shorter all the goddamned time.

We're forced to set up for the night on a slope. That means that it's going to be tough on the guys on the upper part to keep a sharp lookout. It's a very awkward position, trying to face uphill on your belly or on your side without your neck cramping up. Especially in monsoon with the rain whipping you in the face.

But the rain is coming down so hard that we are forced to sit huddled under our poncho liners, knees pressed tightly to our chests, trying desperately to keep warm. It's cold, and the rain seems to be coming down even harder. Nobody's on guard duty. Huddled into ourselves, we try to dream of warmth, but it is impossible. It's as if that word, *warm*, has been removed from the dictionary by the book burners. You remember how to form the letters, how to spell it, pronounce it, but despite all that, it doesn't exist. It's been driven from the world, like a leper, into the shadows, taking with it beloved synonyms such as *hot* and *sizzling* and *scald* and even *torrid* (as in *kiss* or *lovemaking*), and *red-hot* and *scorching* and *blazing*, *smoldering* (a woman, English class, fourth period), and *blazing* and *boiling* and *roasting* (the sweet smell of green chiles on the grill), *flaming* and *blistering*, the opposite of *cold*, *icy*, *freezing*, *chilly*, *frosty*, and *shit*.

Finally, the rain lets up. I stand up to stretch, to move a little, let the blood circulate after being hunched over for too goddamned long. "I'm short, man, short," I'm thinking when I catch some movement out of the corner of my left eye. I turn, and he swings towards me, and for an instant, one long indefinable instant, we stand face to face, no more (and no less) than two feet away from one another. We are brothers, enemies, sons, soldiers, yin and yang, East and West.

I've allowed myself to become totally involved with ridding the word *cold* from existence, of imagining myself (the possibility is becoming more and more real with each passing hour) back into a place long ago known as home; he is involved in getting someplace before nightfall—perhaps he has been thinking of a girl in his village, perhaps his dear old mother, aging father, his newborn child.

His weapon is unslung and mine is lying against my pack, on the ground. Nobody could have possibly seen us in this rain, and, of course, we couldn't have possibly seen anybody either. Unless, of course, either one of us runs right into the other. What the fuck are the odds of that happening out in the middle of a place that has been nicknamed Death Valley? I failed arithmetic in the fourth grade, so I couldn't possibly even come up with a formula that would provide an answer, but I goddamn guarantee the odds would have to be very high, like at least what—five hundred thousand to one? Nobody here would get that lucky at the poker tables or the slot machines in Las Vegas, I goddamn guarantee that. (I'm short, goddammit!) I hit the ground instantly, see the file of soldiers making its way down the hill, each one swinging from the same tree to avoid slipping, sliding down the hill. I turn and see why nobody spotted Charley. Cookie and the rest are still under their poncho liners, facing the same direction as me. I signal them, and when they see the unending file, they freeze. I put my index finger to my lips, urging them to be very quiet, and reach slowly, slowly for my weapon. How they haven't seen us, God only knows.

God is important now. I beg for my life, my prayers never more sincere. All the praying I did back at St. Michael's doesn't amount to shit compared to this. (Oh God, please. *Please*.) The column continues down the hill, like an unending, terrifying centipede.

God. GOD. GOD!

I promise that I will make my life worthwhile, that my life will serve Your purpose. I will never stray from the path of righteousness.

I am shivering uncontrollably. There is nothing, absolutely nothing I can do to make my teeth stop chattering. I have never been and will never again be so terrified. I can't hide it, not even from myself. There is a part of me, way down in the deepest part of me, wailing, "Mother! Mother! Mother!" I can't hide that either.

An infant. Or was that its mother—frightened beyond any measure of fear, wailing?

As soon as they've passed, we move out towards the LZ. Cookie has hung back, providing cover. He cuts loose with a burst of fire and then barks something into the phone. Evidently he's made contact with relay mountain, because he's asking for gunships. Sergeant Gooch crawls to the radio, his map out, and begins calling out coordinates. Cookie cuts loose with another burst, an entire magazine, flicks it free, pounds another one in, locks and loads. It's hard to tell if that stupid peckerwood motherfucker is faking it in order to draw us into a firefight or if he's really seen a gook.

We move to a cluster of dead trees at the edge of the LZ. The gunships are on their way. I can hear the major telling somebody we can walk point when they drop the line company in. That means we're going in after Charley. The major wants a body count before nightfall.

The Cobras arrive, and the sarge gives them the okay for their first run. The first one comes in fast and low, but the grrroaow of the miniguns begins a second or two before the ship passes over us. The rounds hit and rip through the fallen trees, they splatter the mud around us, zip by our heads, missing us by inches and less. Gooch is having a hard time calling them off. He's stuttering, mumbling. He can't get enough saliva to grease his mouth; he's got a super case of cotton mouth, worse than running laps under the hot August sun at the end of the first grueling practice of the football season. Luckily, the second gunship doesn't open fire until it's well beyond us. By the time they come around again for their second run, the sarge is able to tell them not to open up until they get to the wood line. He's gulping down water, gulping and swishing and spitting like a buck private after his first desert skirmish in a French Foreign Legion flick.

The gunships make another run and then buzz around as we secure the LZ, and then the shithooks arrive, full of line doggies. We move out quickly. Too quickly. I don't like walking point for a line company. They move too fucking fast, make too much noise—

give Charley all kinds of time to set up booby traps, time to get ready. The Man says we got to make contact before nightfall.

And we do. Within half an hour. It's possible that Charley is firing and moving back, slowing us down as much as possible so as to give the rest of his company or battalion or whatever time to didi. Or to set up.

I don't know. I can't say. I'll never know if it was already there when we came upon the bunker. It may have been. It must have been. (Maybe I saw the mother place it there. That's possible.) How could anybody have placed it there in the middle of a fire-fight? Right on top of the bunker.

Screaming and wailing.

An infant.

Suddenly I heard the line sergeant call for a guy named Bazooka to get his ass up there on the double, but he got no answer. He hollered again. And again got no response. The line sergeant was cursing madly. Somebody told him that Bazooka was pinned down, and he shouted that he didn't give a shit. He wanted Bazooka to get his ass up there or he was looking at some time in LBJ City. Then he shouted something to Sergeant Gooch, and then Gooch yelled for me, and when I got there he told me I had to go get Bazooka and bring him back. (Why the fuck me? I'm short. Just why the fuck me?) Gooch knows I'm short, the sorry mother-fucker, but that doesn't stop him from asking me if I'm refusing an order. I hear a line doggie screaming his ass off for a medic. The machine gunner in the bunker is smoking us. Somebody yells that the medic's been hit.

Charley's got us by the nuts, and he knows it. We don't know what to do as long as that baby's on top of the bunker. If we dust the baby, he wins, no matter if we wipe out the entire battalion, and another battalion, and another after that. Meanwhile, as we're weighing the consequences, he's ripping us to shreds.

I crawl around until I locate Bazooka. This guy (I'll learn later) can knock off a gnat's balls from as far away as a hundred meters. One look at him, and I know why the sarge sent me after him. And why he didn't answer when the line sergeant called for him.

He's from Mora, one of those little mountain villages an hour or so north of San Miguel. I'm supposed to talk to him, convince him in Spanish to come with me and perform his duty for God and country. I notice his wedding band, and I know—I know from the look in his eyes. He's carrying a picture of his new baby. I don't know what the hell to say to him, and if I did, how to say it. There is nothing I can say or do to spare him. We are compadres and enemigos, both (now) hijos de la chingada madre, greasers and the salt of the earth, putos and paratroopers and wetbacks, both here and back home.

Finally, I ask him if he is from New Mexico. He nods and asks me, "¿Y tú?" We exchange information—where we're from, mutual acquaintances—and promise to get together for a beer back there (and maybe we will if we happen to run into each other, but I don't know that after something like this we're gonna seek each other out). This time of year back home they're opening the compuertas, and the water from the melting snows comes coursing down the acequia madre and into the fields, the beginning of the growing season. We'll both be home to pick and roast and, of course, gorge ourselves on green chile three times and more a day. I tell him I have a can of green chile I'm going to cook with my rice and shrimp rations and share with him tonight. Finally, I say to him that the sergeant wants to see him, and we crawl back towards the bunker.

The machine gunner, a young freckle-faced kid from Missouri named Tom, has managed to crawl close to the sergeant, and when Bazooka is ready with the rocket launcher, the sergeant orders Tom to lay down some fire and give him plenty of cover. The ammo bearer gets ready to feed the belt, and Tom opens up. Bazooka aims, fires, and just as quickly slumps against the ground, his head buried in his arms, motionless.

An infant.

The machine gunner swore it was a girl. Swore all night, softly. All night. After the line company sweeps the area, the sergeant gives Bazooka a hearty thumbs-up, tells him he's gonna recommend him for a Silver Star. "Fuck you," Bazooka tells him, walking off, a raindrop—or is it a tear?—coursing its way steadily down his dirty, hardened face.

It is a curse not only aimed at him but a curse laid on him.

And on you, you masters of war.

And on all your children.

The Man on Jesus Street— Dreaming

The one without a face, the one he shot after his recon squad had been hunted all day, the one he shot after the rain let up, the one without a face was always the last one, and always at dawn—as if his duty was to awaken him 365 days a year, year after year— after only a few minutes of sleep, exactly at 6:15. ▪

The first one, a GI of about nineteen in jungle fatigues, with a shredded leg (the right one), was discovered at 8:15 by Donaldo Martínez (a distant cousin of María Martínez), the head custodian, as he was making his way up the stairs that led to the laundry room. Martínez called security and the emergency room, and the patient was promptly carted around the corner, where he was administered the last rites as the doctors worked on him for over four hours. He had lost a lot of blood on his journey up the hill to the VA hospital.

The admissions clerk had run a check on his dog tags and was totally dumbfounded when he called the chief attending physician, who was equally distressed when he reported to Alberto Martínez (a cousin of the honorable Raymundo Martínez), the head administrator: the young soldier was listed as KIA in Vietnam, near the Cambodian border, on a recon mission in 1967. He had, according to his records, bled to death during monsoon because the medevac had been unable to fly in. He had died three days short of his nineteenth birthday. His parents, in Peru, Indiana, had been contacted and had hung up angrily.

When the clerk wired them, confirming that their son was alive and recuperating at the VA hospital in San Miguel, New Mexico, they caught the first available flight. When Alberto Martínez called Washington, he was told that the VA was sending somebody, a top aide, immediately. Shortly afterward, the CIA, followed by the FBI, called to inform him they were sending a few people to "look into the matter." ▪

Perhaps it was the summer rain that caused him to dream so heavily about JJ and his shredded leg. JJ had moaned all night, losing blood, a splinter of shrapnel in his eye (his left), moaning even while he bit down hard on his olive-green kerchief. He was in unbearable pain. Pain nobody could ever ease or soothe or soften, unspeakable pain made worse with each passing minute, because the more he moved his eye the more it tore.

Perhaps it was the summer rain. From that day on, one thing was certain: JJ disappeared from his dreams. The others, however, persisted.

And always at dawn, always there was the one without a face, more reliable than any alarm clock. ▪

The following night a VC came running at him, and he cut loose with a burst. The gook seemed to hang in midair for minutes as the rounds ripped through him, and then he hit the ground. Then another gook, and another, and another, faster than he could change magazines. And at the end of the long night, the one without a face was there to greet the new day. ▪

There were twenty-three of them, all in black pajamas, with their inner tubes full of rice wrapped around them, some still clutching their AK-47s. Donaldo Martínez called Security immediately and then dialed the emergency room. One of the attending physicians refused to treat the VC, saying that this was a hospital for U.S. veterans only, not for gooks. Donaldo tracked down a cleaning woman in Oncology who was whisked in to translate. A VC with a gut wound, a man named Ngyuen, was demanding treatment, stating he was just as much a victim of American aggression as were the country's own veterans. He had ordered his men to lock and load and had held the security officers to a standoff. Nobody was getting out alive—not the nurses and certainly not the doctors—nobody. They had already survived a firefight with the Albuquerque Police Department's Asian Gang Unit that had been rushed in by chopper, and they had been informed that three SWAT teams had surrounded the building. A hostage negotiator had established phone contact. ▪

The FBI and the CIA were trying to establish whether JJ was telling the truth. The attending physician had been ordered to administer by injection some of the medication provided by the CIA. The Pentagon had begun a complete review of JJ's recon missions in Nam: the dates, locations, and engagements with the enemy. Calls were made to Vietnam to investigate the possibility that JJ had been a prisoner and not KIA and to question Ho Chi Minh City as to whether it was sending sapper squads to the U.S. in order to intimidate Washington into normalizing relations. Agents were already pounding the streets, questioning everybody as they tried to trace the trail of blood left by JJ as far back as possible. ▪

The next morning an entire village stormed into the VA hospital grounds, women clinging desperately to wailing infants, children—some with their clothes on fire—crying desperately for a lost mother, old mama sans searching for their grandchildren, venerable papa sans trying desperately to keep families together, a teenage girl clutching her fiancé's hand. The APD Asian Gang Unit was called in again: The villagers were herded together in the Oncology Ward parking lot, where they remained until nightfall under heavy scrutiny, until the state National Guard was called in. Tents, cots, and cooking facilities were set up and medical attention provided. The cleaning woman from Oncology was happy to be putting in so much overtime, but more than that, she was overwhelmed when she recognized an aunt and several cousins she had presumed had died long ago when the Americans had destroyed their village. ▪

The four tanks rumbled through the gates an hour and a half after the villagers. They had traveled up Martínez Street, not unnoticed but certainly unquestioned, thought to be part of a military training exercise. Nobody seemed to notice the leg tied to the first tank, the arms dangling from the second and the third, and the other leg being dragged along by the last. It wasn't until the following day, when a torso of a young VC, a woman, was discovered and reported to the Asian Gang Unit and then to the FBI, that it was linked to the tanks. And right behind the tanks were the GIs, twenty-five of them, their dicks hanging out, ecstatic with revenge, having not only raped their enemy but ordered the tanks to rev up and head north, south, east, and west. ▪

Just how had he managed to get to the front door of the emergency room, not only blindfolded but with his hands tied behind his back and his dick still wired to the electric circuits of an old G-47 radio that had been given a full crank by the sergeant in charge of intelligence, making him scream secrets about his unit's strengths and movements to the American dogs? ▪

There was, in addition to the one without a face, the infant. And also the brigade of NVA regulars that marched boldly through the gates of the hospital and surrounded the National Guard demanding freedom for the villagers. Henry Kissinger was called in for a quick briefing before catching a flight to Vietnam. The CIA was receiving computer printouts, constantly updated, detailing time, place, and unit for every VC, NVA, and GI in the VA compound, and the FBI had agents around the country searching for other GIs, former VCs, or NVAs who had served in any of these units.

The 101st Airborne was flown in and quickly surrounded the NVAs, claiming twenty-five KIAs and eleven wounded compared to only three KIAs and three wounded in the hour-long battle. The NVA wounded were interrogated—the info fed into the CIA's computer—and then treated.

More FBI agents were ordered in, combing their way down Martínez Street, finding splashes of blood, dried puddles as far

down as The Emporium and then north on Eisenhower to La
Golondrina bar, where some AK-47 rounds were located and
where eyewitnesses pointed them west on Nixon. ▪

Could it be the new medication the psychiatrist had prescribed?
Perhaps he had taken it as directed. He couldn't honestly say.
What he could tell the doctor was that he hadn't felt better since
he had come home—not the cheap whiskey, not the drugs, the
wife he had discarded, the children he had been incapable of car-
ing for—nothing had been able to soothe his pain. Not even putting a gun to his head. Somehow, suddenly, they had disappeared:
the woman who had been tied to the tanks; a hard-core VC they
had captured and turned over for interrogation the morning after
JJ had stepped on a booby trap; JJ had disappeared too, as had the
VC that had come rushing at him night after night; the villagers
with their clothes on fire, parents shouting desperately for lost
children, old papa sans and mama sans barely able to keep up—
they too were gone; the VC with his dick wired to a G-47, who
refused to talk at first but once the interrogator cranked the handle had been willing to give up his mother—he, too, was gone.

Now, only the infant.

And the one whose face he had blown off, who, without fail,
was there to greet the new day, every day. ▪

Vietnam, of course, denied everything. Kissinger reminded
them that he was not, most definitely not, going to play that Paris
Peace Talks shit again. The Vietnamese presented him with documents proving that the entire battalion of NVAs under discus-
sion had been wiped out in a skirmish near the Cambodian border. Kissinger warned them that the U.S. was not, most definitely
not, going to be held responsible for any POWs that had been
listed as KIAs twenty-four years prior to their arrival in the U.S. All
Vietnamese personnel—NVAs, VC, villagers—would be flown
back immediately. Not since Pancho Villa's raid had the U.S.
been invaded. And any more hostile actions would result in a
declaration of war. This was definitely, Kissinger stated in his

most dignified and authoritative manner, not a step towards reconciliation, towards normalizing relations, towards business. A couple more years and the entire POW issue would be laid to rest, once and for all. But this? Just vat the fuck vas this? ▪

He crawled slowly, slowly, hoping the VC would waste him before he got there. Slowly.

But no matter how slowly he crawled, he always found Bazooka. ▪

Sometime during the night, they set up a bunker just outside the perimeter. At first light one of the machine gunners from the 101st spotted one of the gooks slinking back towards the bunker after turning the claymores around so they'd be set off in the direction of the Americans once the VC mounted their attack. The machine gunner opened fire, cutting the gook in half. The bunker returned fire, and three GIs went down.

Half an hour later, the 101st was still pinned down but the VC were running out of ammo. Suddenly, somebody threw a wailing infant on top of the bunker, and immediately the 101st ceased fire. The VC cut down another five GIs before the 101st opened fire again. But they were firing halfheartedly, trying to avoid hitting the infant. The officer in charge called for Bazooka, a nineteen-year-old who just happened to be from Mora, about 180 miles north of San Miguel. Bazooka could knock the balls off a gnat at one hundred meters with a rocket launcher. When he arrived from the opposite end of the perimeter, Bazooka saw the infant and hesitated, hoping that the lieutenant would understand. The VC were expending the last of their ammo furiously, knowing full well they could not lose. They knew they were going to die; they knew the Americans had to finish them, but to finish them they had to kill the infant. The longer the Americans hesitated, the more of them got killed or wounded. They had to kill the infant, and in doing so they would live, but they would also sentence themselves to hell forever. The lieutenant ordered Bazooka to fire. Bazooka aimed. And blew the bunker to pieces. ▪

Now only the man without a face remained. And today was the day that he went to see the psychiatrist to have his medication reviewed. The way things were going, in another week or so the one without a face would be gone, and then he would be allowed to die in peace.

On his way to the bus stop he noticed the two agents walking down Nixon Avenue and then turning left on Jesus Street towards his house. Weird, he thought. The law never went down there on foot.

Security seemed unusually tight at the hospital. He thought he saw Bazooka strapped to a gurney that was being wheeled to the emergency room—but in his camouflage fatigues like he was still in Nam? It had to be the medication. Lately he had sensed JJ and Bazooka around, not just the way you do in a dream but the way you can sense an ambush. There was no way of explaining it. Perhaps the doctor could.

"Feeling great, doctor," he said. They were all gone. All except for the one whose face he had blown off. Yeah, he could describe JJ, but what the hell for? The dude had bought the farm near the border, had bled to fuckin' death, and who gave a shit? Yeah, he remembered how. He had stepped on a goddamn booby trap and bled all the monsoonnight long, a splinter of steel in his eye. Yeah, the dreams of the bunker and Bazooka were gone, too.

But a funny thing. He swore he had seen Bazooka only a few minutes before, still wearing his jungle fatigues. Perhaps the doctor had an explanation for that, because he goddamn for sure didn't.

The villagers, too—gone. And the NVAs and the VC. The tanks. The young girl. Yes, he was doing well. And the one without a face, he asked, he too would go away? ▪

He was certain he had seen JJ in one of the rooms (as certain as he had seen Bazooka), with what were certainly his parents weeping at his bedside.

But the doctor had rushed him into another office where he had been subdued, strapped to a gurney, and rushed into a room where they strapped him into a chair and immediately shot him full of a green medicine that made his heart seem both to slow down and speed up, though the period of rapid pounding seemed so much longer than the other, and pushed a piece of inner tube into his mouth for him to chomp on.

Breathing Them

It occurred to me two or three days ago (I'm no longer sure) exactly twenty-five years to the day (I'm not really sure of that either) that when it really mattered, really counted, the only one I prayed for that day was me.

All that praying I did at St. Michael's—the first thing every morning, the Angelus at noon, before going home, and for all those special intentions—and the only one I could think of to pray for that day was me.

All this occurred to me (of this I am absolutely sure) only after I remembered that right after the rain stopped that night, a blue wind that had originated in China suddenly shifted in a southerly direction straight toward us, and then we were breathing them. ▪

Even the sun came up wet that day.

The same as every or any other day in monsoon: soaked. Shivering.

Certainly not a day for heroism.

A day for staying alive—nothing more.

For a pair of dry socks.

No mud. No hills. No harness straps cutting into your shoulders.

A day for staying inside, in front of a roaring fireplace with a wicked, wild-eyed woman.

Not for sloshing in the mud.

Certainly not a day for being hunted. ▪

This is the question: whether it's better to slosh in the monsoon rain, miserable, or have the rain stop and then sit, soaked, shivering,

perhaps even a little warm if the sun comes out, and have a file of
VC walk right up on you. ▪

Before we knew it they were no more than three feet away,
walking single file down the hill. Perhaps they weren't looking for
us just as we weren't looking for them. The rain had let up. And
we were sitting around, daydreaming. As if the war had suddenly
stopped. Just for us. ▪

Only a little more than an arm's length away. How was it he
didn't see me in that long instant he swung toward me, his rifle
slung listlessly, then grabbed a tree with his free hand, his left, and
continued swinging his way down the mud-slick hill?

And how was it our eyes (his light brown, of that I'm absolutely sure) did not meet? My M16 lying on the ground across my
backpack, useless. ▪

How was it the next one in line didn't see me dropping to the
ground? Didn't see me warning the others.

How was it so many (it could've been fifty, perhaps more—
how many?) of them failed to see so few of us? How many of
them had filed by while the rain was still coming down? So close
we could have (and should have) killed one another without even
bothering to aim. ▪

How can a person be so afraid, trembling already uncontrollably from the cold and now your teeth chattering, and as the file
of left boot, right boot, left continues down the hill, you begin to
pray. You promise (and mean it, God knows) that you will never
sin again. You will walk the righteous path. For the rest of your
days. So afraid you find yourself wishing, unbelievingly, not for
God to come and hold you but for your mother. ▪

Though I prayed (if only for myself) that day, I have since
returned to being the type of Catholic I was before they came
walking by, so it's with hesitancy that I say only God knows

how many had passed while the rain was still coming down and how many after and how it came to pass neither of us saw each other. ■

As soon as the last of the file walked past us, we radioed in for an exfil. Cookie fired at them as we headed for open ground. The Cobras came in, and the sarge called for a run right near the wood line. They opened fire about a hundred yards too soon and nearly wasted us.

Then the chopper came, our prayers answered. But the only open space large enough for an LZ was a nearby mountainside with a steep incline. After several attempts the pilot guided the chopper in close enough for us to jump and grab hold of the strut. But the downdraft and the weight of our packs made it impossible to pull ourselves in. After several futile attempts the door gunner abandoned his M60, unhooked his belt, and hauled Cookie in as we boosted him up. Then the both of them pulled me up. I stood on the strut helping the door gunner haul JJ up, and then JJ and the door gunner pulled the assistant squad leader and then Sarge in.

When we were airborne, Cookie started crying—tears large as monsoon raindrops splashing on the floor of the chopper. While the door gunner was busy, I thought about grabbing the M60 and cutting loose towards the tree line but decided against it. Fate or whatever had allowed us to escape with our lives, and now Charley was escaping with his. ■

We were debriefed. I was so happy to be alive. To have dry socks. I, who had prayed so fervently that day, must have said several more prayers but never thought of uttering even one for them still out there in the rain. I sat down to a hot meal, and then the big guns opened fire. Shortly afterwards the rain stopped. A blue wind that had originated in China suddenly shifted in a southerly direction, straight toward us.

And then we were breathing them. ■

And now you are.

Glossary

DICHOS

Dichos are Spanish sayings and proverbs. In the words of Rubén Cobos, "Proverbs reveal the attitudes, feelings, and psychology of a people." Some of the definitions of the dichos included below are from Cobos's book *Refranes: Southwestern Spanish Proverbs* (Santa Fe: Museuem of New Mexico Press, 1985).

Compuesta, no hay mujer fea.
When she's all decked out, there's no such thing as an ugly woman.

Haciéndose el milagro, aunque lo haga el diablo.
Let the miracle be performed, even if the devil performs it.

Hombre prevenido nunca fue vencido.
A man who is prepared will never be vanquished. Or, forewarned is forearmed.

Ir por lana, y volver trasquilado.
To go for wool, and come back shorn. Or, to set out with a purpose, fail, and return embarrassed.

La mujer y el vidrio, siempre corren peligro.
Women and glass are fragile and always in danger.

Vale más arrear, que no la carga llevar.
Better to be in the driver's seat than to carry the load.

Vale más bien quedada, que mal casada.
Better to have stayed single than to have made a bad marriage.

Vamos a ver, dijó el ciego.
Let's see, said the blind man.

Viejo que se cura, cien años dura.
The old man who takes care of himself lives a hundred years.

Ya que la casa se quema, vamos a calentarnos.
Since the house is burning, let's warm ourselves.

Yo no suelto la cola, aunque me cagen la mano.
I won't let go of its tail, even if I get shit all over my hand. I won't
  give up, even under pressure.

Zorra vieja no cae en trampa.
An old fox doesn't fall into the trap.

WORDS AND PHRASES

Abrazo	Hug
Absolutamente	Absolutely
Acequia madre	Main ditch, aqueduct
Acuérdate	Remember
Alemán, alemana	German
Alma	Soul
Baboso	Jerk
Bésame	Kiss me
Bien	Good, well, truly
Bien loco	Truly crazy
Bienvenido	Welcome
Bonita	Cute
Botas meadas	Pissed-on boots
Buenos días, le dé Dios.	May God grant you a good day.
Buenas noches	Good evening
Cabeza	Head
Cabrón	Son-of-a-bitch, etc.
Cabron(es)	Goat(s)
Cañón	Canyon
Carne seca	Jerky
Chamuscada	Scorched
Charco	Puddle
Chile pequín	Hot chile
Chinelas	Women's shoes, not necessarily fashionable
Chinga'o (chingado)	Frickin'
Chingaso(s)	Punch(es), blow(s)
Chispa(s)	Spark(s), campfire spark(s)
Chorizo	Sausage

Chota(s)	Police officer
Cigarrito	Cigarette
Cobarde	Coward(ly)
Cola	Tail
Como	Like, as
¿Cómo está usted?	How are you? (formal)
¿Cómo hace el gatito?	What sound does a kitty make?
¿Cómo sigue?	How's it going?
Compadre(s)	Close friend(s), godparent(s)
Compuerta(s)	Gate, sluice
Con leche	With milk
¿Cuáles burros?	Which donkeys?
Cuernos	Horns
Desgracia	Misfortune
Diablo bien hecho	Natural-born devil
Didi mau	Get the hell out of here
El Diablo	The Devil
El Dompe Viejo	The Old Dump
El Hombre sin Cabeza	The Headless Man
Enemigo(s)	Enemy, enemies
Entonces	Then
Era	Was
Es cierto	It's true, certain
Es verdad	It's true
Esto	This one
Golondrina	Swallow
Gracias a Dios!	Thank the Lord!
¡Hay que laureles tan verdes!	Oh what beautiful laurels (flowers)!
Si pienas abandonarme,	If you're thinking of leaving,
mejor quitar me la vida.	better to take my life.
Hijo(s) de la chingada madre	Sonsabitch(es)
Hombre	Man
Hoy	Today
Huevos	Eggs

Iglesia	Church
Jito	Son (short for *hijito*)
Jodido	One who is screwed
Ladron(es)	Thief, thieves
Lambe	Kiss-ass
L'otro	The other one
Llano	Plain, prairie
Llanta	Tire
María Purísima	Virgin Mary
Más o menos	More or less
Masa	Dough
Matanza, la	The killing
Mea'o (meado)	One who has peed on himself
Melon(es)	Melon(s)
Mente	Mind
Menudo	Tripe soup
Mera, mera, la	The top one, the boss, the person with brains
Mierda	Crap
Milagro	Miracle
Mira	Look
Moco(s)	Booger(s)
Mosca	Fly
Nalgas	Buttocks
Navaja	Knife
Nicho	Niche
No más	No more
Padre Nuestro	Our Father
Pala(s)	Shovel(s)
Pan tosta'o	Toast
Panzón	Big-bellied

Pedo	Fart
Pendejo, pendejada	Idiot, idiotic
Pero	But
Pinche	Tough, jerk, idiot
Pobrecito	Poor little one
Político(s)	Politician(s)
Poquito	A little bit
Primo	Cousin
Promesa	Promise
Pues	Then
Puntillas	Tacks
Puto, puta	Prostitute
Que	That, which
¿Qué no?	Is this (that) not true?
Querido	Dear
Quién sabe cuando	Who knows when
Refrán	Saying, proverb
Sabroso(s)	Delicious
Sapo	Toad
Seguro que	Certain that, definitely
Sí	Yes
Simón	Cool slang for "yes"
Sinvergüenza	Shameless ones
Sin vergüenza	Unashamedly
Sonamabisquete	"Son-of-a-biscuit," or a nonsense word used as an expletive
Suegra	Mother-in-law
También	Also
Te digo	I tell you
Toma, m'hito, aquí tienes dos reales.	Here's a couple of nickels, my son (archaic measurement of money).
Tirar tripas	To throw up
Tragito	Sip

Truchas	Cool it! Hey! Watch out!
Tú sabes	You know
Turista	Tourist
Vecino	Neighbor
Velorio	Wake
Ven (venir)	Come
Vengan a comer	Come and eat
Víbora, viborita	Snake
Yerba mala	Bad weed, marijuana
Yo creo Dios mío, que estás en el altar . . . Bendito sea Dios!	I believe, my Lord, that you are up there on the altar. . . . Blessed be God!
¿Y qué?	So what?

Quintana follows Mosco Zamora, a World War II veteran, and Johnny Barros, a Vietnam veteran, through haphazard collisions of fantasy and reality in small-town New Mexico and beyond. Quintana's eloquence as a poet infuses his candid and imaginative narration of stories drawn from both his own life and the tales spun by his father-in-law, a native of Silver City, New Mexico.